Still Into You

A Novel

Emme Burton

Still Into You
Emme Burton
Copyright 2014

Editor: Sharon Korn
Cover Design: © Sarah Hansen, Okay Creations.
Formatting: Polgarus Studio
Author Photograph: Dana Colcleasure

DEDICATION

To ALL the Readers out there.

Not just of my books, but any books. Those that stick to one genre and those that like to mix it up. Thank you for loving books and supporting authors.

And of course, to my family-BC, Thing One, Thing Two and J-Dog. After all this time, I'm STILL into you.

Still Into You Playlist

Cool by Gwen Stefani

Like a G6-Far East Movement

Closing Time-Semisonic

Every Breath You Take-The Police

Home, Sweet, Home-Motley Crue

You're My Favorite Waste of Time-Marshall Crenshaw and The Handsome, Ruthless and Stupid Band

Look What You've Done-Jet

Say Something I'm Giving Up On You-Great Big World

Closer to the Edge-30 Seconds to Mars

By Myself-Linkin Park

Still Into You-Paramore

I Choose You-Sara Bareilles

Happy-Pharrell Williams

Crazy Lucky-Better Than Ezra

Chapter 1-Past: 3 ½ years ago

"The state calls to the stand, Elizabeth Connelly Brandon," the bailiff announces.

I'm a witness in the case against Neil Ireland, in one of the biggest court cases to hit the metro area in a long time. Neil Ireland, a man who, at one time, I believed to be my boyfriend. But as he has repeatedly stated in police interviews, "It was never like that." Neil is being tried for sexual assault, the production and distribution of pornography, and the transportation of minors across state line for both. I'm the last witness of five women. Well, one woman – me – and four teenage girls. The girls each testified and told stories similar to mine, except in one case, where the girl's father found her in time, was able to get her to the hospital and tested. Tested for assault. Which was positive via the rape kit. And for drugs, namely Rophynol – also positive. Getting that objective evidence, according to the prosecuting attorney, is what will probably put Neil away. So why am I testifying? To make the case stronger. To show a pattern of behavior that has been ongoing. And I have become the "face" of the victims in this case. The court is closed to photography and filming. Reporters can be present, but no sketches of any of the women are allowed, except me. The other victims are all underage. Their names and faces are being kept from the public. I, on the other hand, am an adult. This isn't an accident. The prosecution wants a real person to whom the public can relate. Me.

I walk to the witness stand as calmly as I can. I know when I turn around I will have to look into the eyes of the man that used and violated me. Some may not see it that way, but I'm here to make them understand. When I finally get up to the stand, I turn and see him – Neil Ireland. He is dressed conservatively, as am I. That's what happens when you are a defendant or witness, you're dressed to present the image your attorney wants you to portray. Neil has on khakis, a blue oxford shirt and a navy sport coat... something he'd never wear when I knew him. Preppy. He is still handsome. It's just a fact. I've heard he receives love letters in jail from women who don't know the monster he really is.

I'm sworn in by the bailiff and sit in the witness stand. After the brief glance at Neil, I know I can't look at him again, so I swiftly pin my gaze to the face in the gallery that I know is always on my side. My husband, my rock, Davis. We talked about it before we came to the courthouse today, and made a plan. I'm going to answer all my questions like I'm talking to him.

The prosecuting attorney approaches and asks me, "Ms. Brandon, how long have you known the defendant, Mr. Ireland?"

"About three years."

He continues, "And what, Ms. Brandon, was the nature of your relationship?"

I pause and then answer slowly, like I've been coached, "At first, we were colleagues, I guess you'd say. We were both Resident Assistants, RAs, at Weldon University. Then..." I begin to stammer a bit, "We, well, I thought he became my boyfriend...but I guess..."

"Objection!" Neil's attorney yells out, "Speculation."

The judge agrees, "Sustained."

My head is spinning at the rapid-fire interaction and lawyer speak.

The prosecuting attorney tells the judge, "I'll rephrase," and then he turns his attention back to me, "Ms. Brandon, you said 'at first' your relationship with Mr. Ireland was as co-workers."

"Yes." I say, a little more tentative now.

"Can you describe, without labeling, how your relationship changed?"

This next part is hard. My husband, his parents, and MY parents are all watching. I've told all of them this story before, but here in court, with others watching and reporters writing, it's mortifying. It's a good thing I've been able to see Dr. Matt, my psychologist, more often, now that he's moved to St. Louis.

I tell the whole story, with only a few objections and redirections. I describe Neil pursuing me after knowing me casually for about a year and how he actively seduced me. Elaborating on how our relationship became sexual and almost compulsive on my part was humiliating.

"I thought he loved me," I said.

I knew it had to be said to support the other girls' testimony. Their experience sounded much worse than mine. I revealed how Neil Ireland drew me in and then, after announcing that I was merely a "plaything," dumped me at his brother Randall's house and had no contact with me again until he was arrested over a year later. The prosecuting attorney allows me to describe my time at Randall's house, but only to a point. Enough to paint the picture that it was no mistake I'd wound up with Randall. That I was set up to be moved in with Randall for purposes of eventually filming me during sexual acts. It's the same modus operandi the other girls described in their testimony. I really don't know how I'm keeping myself from vomiting or passing out, the recollection is so painful.

I'm looking back and forth between the light on the ceiling and Davis' compassionate eyes during the reveal of these most degrading memories. I feel his support and empathy for me across the room. When the prosecutor asks me if I have any memories other than passing out in Randall's house and waking up naked with a video camera in the room, the defense attorney objects again. The judge agrees and the questioning is halted. Evidently, neither side wants me saying more about Randall. I know it's because if he is ever caught there are similar charges pending against him, along with the assault of Davis and me under the bridge. I feel as if I'm going through it all over again – my time with Neil, whatever happened with Randall...all of it. And again, I can't remember the most important part. What exactly happened to me in Randall's house? Was I drugged? Was I raped? Is there a video out there of me? Porn?

Strangely, the defense has no questions for me. I'm dismissed by the judge and get down from the stand. As I pass by the prosecutor, he whispers, "Good job, Biz."

I say nothing.

I don't look at Neil as I pass by him. I just keep my eyes on Davis. I never want to have to see Neil Ireland again. I've wished it so many times before, but maybe this time, he'll be put away and I won't have to. Davis stands and pushes his way past his parents to meet me in the aisle of the court's gallery. We walk out of the court together. I don't want to stay and listen to any more testimony. I have to remain available in case I'm needed for further questioning, but I don't have to stay in the courtroom. I can go home and be called back in for as long as the case continues.

The minute we move through the courtroom doors, I hear the whirr of digital cameras and questions being "whisper-shouted" in my direction. Reporters that couldn't get into the courtroom and all of the photographers are there – waiting for me. Davis wraps his arm around my waist, knowing it's too much for me. I keep my head down and move where he leads me, navigating us through the crowd. The questions coming at me sound like drunken voices in a sea of white noise, and make no sense to me. My vision blurs, and I am getting overheated. Davis senses this in me. In moments, we are in quiet, in a small room with light green walls. Davis places me in a hard-backed chair at a table and squats in front of me. I sit, stunned, with my head down.

"Biz? Baby, are you all right?" Davis' voice is so gentle. He holds my hand and reaches up to cup my face, moving it slightly to look at him. "You were so brave. So very brave. Not one tear. How did you do that?"

He doesn't care about what I just put out there for the whole world to know, only how I am.

I launch myself into his arms and he takes my full weight easily. I'm no longer in the chair, but sitting on the floor with Davis. I still don't cry.

"I really, I don't know… I just had to get it all out, as much as they would let me. I had to be strong, because, those other girls, they're so young and they went through everything I did, more even. I've cried enough about this. Now, I just want it to be over. I want something positive to come out of this." I explain. With Davis holding me, I feel better. Stronger.

My attorney, Anne Walker, enters the small witness preparation room and stops short, seeing Davis and me on the floor, embracing.

As Davis helps me up and we both sit back at the table, she asks, "Is everything okay?" We both nod our heads yes and Davis reaches over to take my hand. Anne continues, "Biz, you did well. I made a statement to the reporters that you only wished to see justice served and that you will be giving an interview once the trial is over."

Anne is a take-charge spitfire of an attorney. Davis' parents found her for me, once we knew I would be called to testify. Anne is seeing me through all of my dealings with the police, the legal system and the media. She and I agree that after the trial I'll be giving the interview to Gail Patton, my boss on KTTA, the station I work for.

"What do I do now?" I ask.

Anne sits across from me at the table. "Let's wait for the next recess. Your family can leave then and we should know if the court will need you any more today. I don't think they will, but you never know. If they don't, you can go home. I'll keep you apprised of how the case is going."

I sigh audibly, releasing hours, if not days and weeks, of tension.

Anne senses my relief and tells me, "Biz, you did a good thing in there. I know it's been hard on you and Davis, and your families, but you did the right thing by sharing your story."

"Thank you, Anne. Thank you both," I squeeze Davis' hand a little tighter. All I want to do is go home.

***

At the conclusion of the next recess, court is dismissed for the day. After many hugs and words of love and support, Davis' parents are headed back home to Illinois. They have been great through this whole trial. My mother-in-law, Meredith Brandon, who was once very frosty toward me, is now firmly in my corner. My mother, Diane, has not let go of my hand the entire trip home from the courthouse. I'm sitting in between Davis and her in the back seat of our Lexus SUV, holding hands with both of them. We aren't talking, just *being*.

My parents are staying with Davis and me until the proceedings are over. It's put a damper on our sex life, but so has the trial. Davis has been very understanding. No, not just understanding. Patient. A saint.

When we get home and my mother finally lets go of me, after one more hug, I take myself to the en-suite bathroom in the master bedroom. I climb out of my courtroom clothes – white shirt, black suit, conservative black pumps, small diamond stud earrings – and take a bath. I want to wash off the bad parts of today and the past three years. Only the bad parts.

Davis enters the bathroom with a glass of white wine. I can tell it's nice and cold by the condensation bubbling up on the outside of the glass. He takes a sip and then hands it to me in the tub.

"I thought you might need this," he says.

"I do. Thank you." I say and take a long drink. I don't drink much. I'm not good at it, but tonight I think I could use it. After taking another couple sips, I tell him an idea that's been bouncing around in my head all afternoon. "Davis, I'd like to do something. Something to help victims of…victims of situations like I've been in, like those girls have been in. Something that educates for prevention, but also supports them afterward. What do you think?"

Davis takes another drink of the wine, almost finishing it. Looks like he needed it, too. "Like what?" he asks.

I shrug, "I don't know yet, but something. Something for teenagers, young adults? Maybe not just girls. Maybe educate about mental illness." I take a deep breath and say it, "Something that could have helped someone like… Cole."

Cole. Davis' brother who committed suicide and accidentally shot Davis' father leaving him paralyzed. It's the thing that changed Davis

6

forever. We don't say Cole's name out loud too often. Davis' lips press into a tight line. I can sense pain and sadness in that tiniest of expression changes.

"I'm going to talk to Anne about it and Gail Patton at the station. As much as I… we want to, we can't just pretend these things never happened. We have to turn it into something positive," I say, finishing my proposal.

Davis hands me the last bit of wine and I down it. I can feel the small bit I've had relaxing me along with the warmth of the bath water.

Davis looks down at me and smiles, a proud but tired smile. "So brave," he whispers. He leans down, takes the wine glass from my hand and kisses me on the hair. "Whatever you want or need to do, Lizard Breath, I'm with you. I'm always with you."

"Thanks, Mavis." Using his nickname, I smile up at him sweetly and then watch him, all of him, as he turns and leaves me to soak some more.

***

Neil Ireland was sentenced to twenty years in jail for sexual assault and statutory rape. There was not enough evidence to convict him of the manufacturing of porn. Jurors interviewed afterward revealed they believed that Neil Ireland was the predator and procurer of the girls for the reported pornography, but they didn't see proof that he was directly involved in the making of it. My experience seems to fall in line with that thinking. Neil seduced and had sex with potential, candidates – naïve like me – for Randall's pornography business, finding them wherever he was at the time. Neil found me in college. When he went into teaching he switched to high school girls. Once he was through with them, through "grooming" them, Neil would give them to Randall. It all made sense to me now, and evidently to the jury as well. Any future pornography charges would be laid on Randall Ireland. Randall is still at large and has not been heard from in the months since he beat Neil with a baseball bat and pistol-whipped Davis in a skatepark under the South Kingshighway bridge.

I never have to see Neil again, but Randall is still out there.

My contact at the metro St. Louis police department, Detective Donovan Garrett, gives me regular updates. Randall seems to have vanished off the face of the Earth. Part of me prefers it that way – he can just stay gone and out of our lives. Another part waits, wondering when he'll show up again. I also wonder if I'll ever get answers to what happened to me. It's a frequent topic in sessions with Dr. Matt.

***

Dr. Matt taps his pen on the arm of his chair and leans slightly forward toward me. "Why do you expect yourself to remember, Biz? *You* weren't there."

I shake my head, confused by his statement. "Of course I was. I was in that room. I called my dad, passed out... I... I remember waking up, no clothes, sprawled on the bed on my stomach... I remember the tripod, the camera... I just can't remember, couldn't tell what I'd... what Randall had, you know, *done* to me. I *was* there."

Still leaning forward, Dr. Matt proceeds to elucidate me about what he means by "not there." "Biz, physically you were there, but I suspect you'll never remember. If I'm right and you *were* drugged, you will probably never recall ..."

"But," I protest.

"Just hear me out. Have you ever had surgery?"

I give him a look and tell him "Sure." I had my tonsils out when I was ten.

Dr. Matt asks flatly, "Do you remember surgery?"

Somewhat irritated I answer, "Yes, I remember being wheeled in and when I woke up my throat was on fire. I was given ice chips to suck."

Trying to bring me back on point, the good doctor stops me, "That wasn't the question, Biz. The question was, 'Do you remember the surgery?' "

Instantaneously, I blurt out sarcastically, "Of course not. I was under anesthes...i...a." And as that word tumbles out of my mouth, Dr. Matt's reasoning finally hits me. "Are you saying I was drugged THAT much?"

The doctor nods, pressing his lips together and raising his eyebrows in silent confirmation. He finally speaks, "I think it's possible you were. You see, after a surgery you won't recall the actual procedure or you would have memory of the pain. Your retelling of the events of that night with Randall are similar to your surgery experience. Beginning. End. No middle and no recall of it. And other than the frustration of not knowing, there is no recollection of the act or of pain."

He's right. I don't remember any physical pain or feeling "used" down there. I don't remember Randall touching me, only threatening me verbally. I only have Neil's word about a video. I think back to Randall's plan to take me with him when he escaped the police. Wanting to "own" me. Possess me. Steal me from Davis.

When I relay to Dr. Matt about Neil and Randall's behavior and the supposed video, we both sit in silence for a moment.

Dr. Matt finally speaks, "Have you ever considered, Biz…" I know what he's thinking even as he talks, "…since you have never seen a video…that maybe there isn't one? Or that maybe there is, but someone doesn't want to share it, because maybe they are…"

Neil's words at the skatepark flood back into my consciousness. *"Oh, Biz, still so naïve. There is no video. I mean there is, but I don't have it. Randall is a complete freak about that video. He won't even show it to me. I have no idea where it is or what he did with you. God knows I'd love to."*

Dr. Matt and I say the word at the same time, "Obsessed."

At this moment Randall, although not seen for months, seems more of a threat than I ever imagined. If he is obsessed, is he really as "gone" as we all think?

Chapter 2-Present: Friending Jake

Closing the door to our condo and turning to face it as I shut and lock it for the night, I exhale any residual anxiety from the evening. It really wasn't that bad – seeing Jake. Cathartic, actually. Closure, if you will. Before I can even turn around, I hear the TV click off in the bedroom. Davis. My husband. Love of my life. He's right where he was when I left, or so he would have me believe. I know him pretty well after five years together. He'll be sitting upright on our bed, with his legs stretched out in front of him, reading or messing around on his iPhone, trying to act nonchalant. I know he is anything but. He's probably been glued to his phone and pacing like a tiger in a zoo enclosure. He hates when I'm away from him and I feel the same way. Especially tonight, when I went out without him to see an old (sort of) boyfriend. Davis and I are just better when we're together.

Davis must have heard the door close. He shouts out a greeting, "Hey Baby, you're back," quickly followed by a question, "How was it?" *How was it?* I ponder the question and how I will respond as I make my way to the French doors to our bedroom. It doesn't matter what I say, Davis won't like it. He was not pleased at my decision to go and meet with Jake Gianni. Jake was my boyfriend at Weldon University, right before Davis and I fell in love. He was actually Davis' friend first, but, at the time, he turned out to be, well, an asshole. Putting it bluntly, Jake was just on a mission to bang me. That's it. He may have liked me a little, but, really, he knew I'd been with a certain guy before I met him and I was...how do I put this... "enthusiastic" when it came to sex with that guy, and Jake wanted some for himself. That guy was Neil Ireland. Now convicted felon Neil Ireland. But Jake, he never had me. All he got for his efforts at bedding me was a beat down from Davis. So when Jake contacted me on Facebook, asking to be friends, Davis was naturally pissed. I explained to Davis that I wanted to give Jake a second chance to prove he was a decent person. Maybe he had changed. We talked it over a lot and I eventually friended Jake. That was okay. I could handle that. I can handle way more now than I could five years ago. I still always want to trust. Davis still feels I'm too trusting. After chatting on Facebook for a few months, Jake asked me to go have coffee to talk in person. Again, Davis wasn't thrilled, but supported my decision to go meet Jake. He told me if I felt uncomfortable or unsafe at any point to leave or call him and he would come get me.

I walk into the bedroom and hang my purse on the back of the desk chair. I pull off my diamond earrings and throw them in my jewelry box. I should probably be more careful with my jewelry. Even without looking, I can tell Davis is in exactly the position I thought he'd be on the bed, watching me. The TV isn't off, it's on CNN and muted. I haven't turned to look at him yet. Taking off my watch and, this time, placing it in the jewelry box, I tell him, "It was weird… at first… and then… fine. No drama." I can't wait to get out of my street clothes and into my jammies. As I pull my t-shirt over my head, I turn to face Davis and give him a smile to let him know it went okay… maybe also to tease him a bit. I can tell by the way a mischievous smirk appears on his face and one of his eyebrows arches that I have his attention, at least physically, now.

I pull my t-shirt all the way off and continue to tell him about the meeting with Jake, "He's… sweet." Davis' sexy smirk morphs to a frown. "and really a little sad. He's had two failed marriages and no kids." No kids… just like us, I think to myself with a mental sob. I quickly shake off the thought and continue, "He apologized about 20 times in the course of an hour. How he was so sorry if he hurt me. How he couldn't believe what an ass he was, cheating on me. All I could say was, 'Hey, it's fine. It was so long ago. Things are the way they are supposed to be now.' He shook his head like he didn't agree."

Davis' eyes are on me. He hasn't said a word, but I can feel a tension coming off him. Something between anger and desire. I have a habit of chattering in a squirrel-like fashion that I know turns Davis on. That's probably what's happening, since I've been doing all the talking. I have to admit, I'm feeling the need to pounce him. Who's the tiger, now?

I slip off my capris and walk around the room in my bra and panties. After depositing my t-shirt and capris in the hamper, I stretch. The lengthening and relaxing of my muscles releases more tension, but I'm not just doing it for my benefit. Davis is still watching me closely, processing my words about Jake and, if I know him, working hard to not think about the other man that hurt me... and him. The one that isn't a Facebook friend or in jail. The one still on the loose – Randall Ireland. Maybe I can take his mind off of that.

Davis finally speaks, and when he does it comes out in a low, spine-tingling growl, "Jake still wants in your panties."

I think my distraction techniques have worked. "What, these?" I reply coyly, while popping my black boy short-covered booty toward him, looking over my shoulder and snapping at the bottom of both sides of said boy shorts by reaching around behind with both my index fingers. I continue toward the master bathroom, trying to act cool and not like I'm completely dying to touch him (which I am, so I guess I still have a few acting chops in me) when Davis lunges toward me, grabs my arm and forcefully pulls me over to him on the bed.

He growls again, "Grrr, It... Kills... Me... when you do that."

Any attempt at retaining my "faux aloof" attitude is lost and I sigh huskily, "Tell me about it, Mavis."

Davis doesn't say a word, but he certainly "tells me about it." He has me straddling him, still in his TV watching position. But he's not watching TV now. Davis reaches over to the bedside table and with a quick flick of his wrist, grabs the remote and turns the television off completely. His hands are both back on me in a flash, his thumbs at my hipbones, fingers and palms cupping my ass. He digs his fingers in first and then his thumbs, facilitating a rocking motion of my most sensitive area against his rough jeans that are straining against the hardness of his already developed erection. It feels delicious and all the friction is making me slick up. I hum aloud and run myself down the full length of him. Davis' hands move from my hips and wander slowly, purposefully, side by side up my stomach. He spreads his fingers to encompass most of my torso in his touch. His hands eventually reach my breasts, which now feel fuller and almost pulsing. Davis cups them both and runs his thumbs roughly across my taut, needy nipples over my black satin bra. Still grinding into him for more, I arch my back and push my breasts further into his hands. It's not enough. I want more. So does Davis, and in the seconds it takes me to reach around and unhook my bra, he has divested me of it and chucked it across the room. I hear it smack against a wall on impact. His hands are back on me in an instant, continuing their mission. Davis rolls one of my nipples between his thumb and forefinger, extending it, almost to the point of pain. It's an exquisite sensation that shoots lower into my core, increasing my want. I'm having a hard time focusing, but need Davis to be less clothed. Now.

I manage to reach down for the bottom of his t-shirt and just before yanking it up, smile at the words on the front of it, CAT LOVER. Cat Lover? Ooooh. I get it. Cat. Lover. As in the cat that every woman has. I smile even bigger. My grin must be a like a green light to Davis, because he lurches forward as I tug up on the shirt, and once again pulls my hips down on his. As his shirt comes off I'm rewarded with the sight of his hard, straining abdominal and chest muscles as he comes toward me, reaches around my waist and pulls me down on top of him, finally skin to skin.

Davis doesn't allow it for long. He rolls me to my back and brings his face close to mine, but he doesn't kiss me. No. He inhales and then kisses my forehead, my eyebrows, eyes, temples, cheeks, near my ears, everywhere but my mouth. Davis kisses under my ear and then with a flattened tongue, licks me slowly from there to my collarbone. He kisses all the way across, stopping to pay extra attention with more licking to the place where I was once injured. He slides slowly down to my breasts and gives each one, in turn, the Davis treatment. I groan in anticipation. When his lips finally encircle a nipple, his tongue laves it and he sucks powerfully as I build exponentially.

One of my hands is in his silky dark brown hair, rubbing strands of it between my fingers as I pull him in, begging for more. My other hand is at his waist, working fretfully to unbutton and remove his jeans. It's tricky, one-handed. I say a silent thank you that he has already taken his belt off and then one aloud when I see he is not wearing boxers. I believe the actual words are, "Commando! Thank you." All Davis does is smile. I don't see it, but I can feel it as his lips leave my nipple ever so briefly.

My hand encircling his warm hardness, I try to slide down and move him onto my slickness, while tipping my head down to kiss his hair and encourage Davis to look up and kiss me. He is having none of that. In fact, Davis is heading in the other direction. Before I know it, Davis IS looking up at me, but from a lower viewing area, at the apex of my thighs. He winks one of his dazzling green eyes at me, dips his head and moans with pleasure above my now only-too-ready core. Just his breath washing over my sensitive folds starts the flood. Davis luxuriously licks up and down. He is managing my need, not letting me move to the next level too fast or too slow. Davis' tongue eventually arrives at my clit and after circling it slowly a few times, lingering under the hood and giving a bit more pressure there, he begins his assault. I know he uses the "alphabet method" at times down there and if that's what he's doing now, he's never going to get to LMNOP, because... I... I...

A swirl of colors dance behind my closed eyelids, my whole body shakes and my core and thighs contract and release. Davis doesn't stop, he actually sucks my whole clit more intensely. The gripping down low powers up and the sequence of colored lights begins again. I pant wildly, pull at the sheets and then pound on Davis' back, my actions asking him to stop and NEVER stop at the same time. As I whimper and try to put together a thought, I open my eyes. Davis' incredible smile is right in front of me and he kisses me, with the same skill he did moments ago, but lower. It's enough to start the colored lights again. I reach down and stroke his now seriously hard erection. I don't know if he can wait any longer, but I can't, and he has been very patient and attentive to...the Cat.

Cat Lover. God, Davis kills me.

I bring him up and rub the head of his cock over my wet and vibrating core, then I release him as he slides into me and holds still for just a moment. I contract lightly around him and it's like a silent signal. Go time.

Davis slides in and then back out with measured strokes, until we are both covered in a thin veil of sweat. There is now no way to control, prevent, delay. We thrust and rock violently, each urging the other for more. I know I am close again. Davis seems to sense it. I feel him take a huge breath and growling loudly into my hair, he spills into me. His guttural release opens the floodgates for a third time for me and we drown in one another, shouting unintelligible pleas for mercy.

Oh yeah, "He told me about it."

Three times.

***

I wake up before Davis. Something I rarely do, but when it happens, it's a treat. He looks so relaxed, lying on his stomach, arms up under the pillow, his mussed up hair framing his face, which is turned toward me. I reach over and with two fingers, rub a piece of his hair near his ear and push it back away from his face. His hair is not as long as when we first met, but not the shortest it's been either. No matter. He could be bald and I would be in his spell. But I would miss his hair.

I think back to last night. The unpleasant things that kept creeping into my thoughts, how I distracted myself and Davis to make us both feel better. It worked. I definitely felt, *feel* better, but as I think back through the evening, I'm stopped when I recall the words, 'No kids' and how in the moment I thought about us with –no kids, and then with a sigh, while still gazing at Davis, I say it aloud, flatly, "No Kids."

The contemplation of those two words make me antsy, and as quietly as I can, I find my panties and Davis' rumpled CAT LOVER t-shirt in the bed, stand up and put them on. I tiptoe into the kitchen and get a cup of coffee, which thankfully, Davis set up last night to brew automatically. He's considerate like that. The coffee making, it's his "thing." I always make sure to tell him its better when he makes it. It's become a family joke. Family. Our tiny two-person family.

After pouring myself a cup of coffee and fixing it up just the way I like it, with two sweeteners and lots of milk, I pad back toward the bedroom. When I get to the open French doors, I lean for a minute against the door jamb and look at my bedroom, my bed and the sexy, generous man lying there. The sheets are only covering the bottom half of him, leaving his back and just the top of his ass deliciously viewable. I really am a very lucky girl. I tell myself that very thing, but still can't shake the weird, somewhat irritable mood I have this morning. Not able to go back to bed, as I'm now wide awake, but also not ready to start my day, I make my way into our large walk-in closet. Before I'm even aware, I notice that I'm doing the thing I do when I need to calm and think. I organize. It's a strange meditative process that I will do almost automatically when I'm trying to piece through a challenge. NOT cleaning, organizing.

Today, Davis' sock and t-shirt drawers are the lucky winners of my attention. Placing my coffee mug on a safe place on the floor of the closet, I pull out the drawers and dump all of their contents out on the floor – socks on the left, t-shirts on the right. I'm about to make my nest in between, when I stop myself and walk back into the bedroom to retrieve my iPhone and earphones. Coffee, music, sorting – a strange way to get Zen, but it works for me. I pause and take another look across the bed at my still-sleeping husband. I can't help thinking what a great dad he would be and, if our kids were fortunate, how they would look like him. It's so easy to go back to that place, but I shake it off again, knowing that dream will probably never come true. I go back to my nest in the closet.

Sitting cross-legged on the floor of the closet, surrounded by apparel, I am nearly finished sorting all of Davis' socks, throwing out the worn ones and pairing up the rest into sock balls, when my nest is disturbed. I jump slightly as Davis comes up behind me and sits, his front to my back, his legs straddling mine. He takes one of the earphones out and, I'm guessing, puts it in his ear. I'm listening to Imagine Dragons, an acoustic version. Davis wraps his arms around my waist and, leaning into me, turns his head and presses his cheek against the back of my left shoulder. I can feel his hair, his warm skin and a few light kisses.

In a not-quite-awake voice he asks, "Whatcha doin' in here? I woke up and you were gone."

"Organizing" I reply. Davis already knows what "organizing" means. When he first met me, I used to chant a mantra and put myself in a self imposed "time-out" when I was anxious or panicky. I don't need to do that very often any more, thanks to my work with my counselor, Dr. Matt. I manage my anxiety more proactively now. Oh, I still chant when needed, but less often. Now I find more useful outlets – like organizing. Or as Dr. Matt puts it...

Davis finishes my thought by saying, "Using your anxiety for good, instead of evil?"

I laugh softly and relax into his firm, warm chest, resting my head back on his shoulder. "Yes," I answer quietly. Davis' presence is as calming as organizing, at times. "I'm whipping your socks and t-shirts into shape."

"Thank god," Davis says with low chuckle, "They were getting unruly."

"Well, the socks are done. Look through these t-shirts with me. Some of them are looking a little threadbare and shabby."

I can feel Davis shaking his head against my back. "You do know this is a weird couple activity, right?"

"It's not weird, it's normal, everyday...I like it."

I hold up Davis' t-shirt that says, "It's All Fun and Games Until Someone Posts the Video." I thought it was funny the first time I saw it, but it always gave me an uneasy feeling at the same time. Now I know why.

I must have frowned because Davis snatches it from my hands, "We're getting rid of this one right now. It's not even funny." Davis balls it up and throws it in the trash. "No shirts that don't make you smile. That's the rule." I can't argue with his new rule. I simply nod my head in agreement.

I'm rifling through the rest of his shirts, folding and piling, when I come across a green t-shirt I never really noticed before. I wonder why?

"What's this?" I flatten the shirt out to read the text scrawled artistically across the top of the shirt, very close to the neckline.

I read it out loud, "An Awkward Morning Beats a Boring Night." I chuckle, but don't smile. I've probably mindlessly folded it dozens of times, but I've never seen Davis wear it.

Davis explains, "God, that shirt is so old. I stopped wearing it after we met. Like, the day after we met. I was done with awkward mornings." Davis must have picked up on my lack of smile.

I confess, "You know, before, I would have laughed my ass off at that shirt. I hope I'm not losing my sense of humor."

Davis treats the green shirt the same as the 'video' shirt, balling it up and trashing it. "You still have it. You still like innuendo. Look at all the shirts you've let me keep." He indicates the large pile of shirts with all of his funny, slightly dirty sayings. "These two just don't work anymore."

"Yeah, I still like 'Google' and 'Cat Lover.'"

Davis pulls me back toward him and rains kisses in my hair. "See? How about 'Protect Your Nuts.'" It's the shirt with a squirrel holding up a big stick on it.

"That one, too, " I admit and turn my face to kiss his lips.

"Yeah, it reminds me of your chatter."

My mood lightens as we make out like teenagers on the closet floor.

***

"You didn't tell me what caused to you to attack my sock and t-shirt drawers so violently," Davis queries me, without directly asking a question. He's not looking at me. I'm sitting at the bar in our kitchen and he's cooking breakfast. I can't see his whole face, only his profile.

"I was thinking about something I told you last night about Jake."

Davis' expression doesn't change, he still focuses on his pancake making and asks, "What's that?"

"No Kids." I just bluntly put it out there. "Just like us."

Davis scoops two pancakes onto a plate, turns off the burner and puts down his spatula. He places it in front of me.

Davis fixes onto me with his sparkling green eyes, "I was wondering if that's what you were thinking about. You were unusually nonchalant when you said that last night. I know you don't take it lightly."

"I… I really thought I was fine. Like I'd cried my last tear about us not being able to get pregnant, but… it still hurts. I don't think it will ever not hurt. You'd be such a great dad. I feel like I'm robbing you of that chance."

Davis walks around the bar, spins me on my barstool to face him and pulls me close, wrapping my legs around his waist. "Lizard, I. Love. You. You! I married you for you, not any other reason. I'm a very happy man. Would I love to have a kid? Sure. Only because he or she would be half you. YOU! Am I making it clear enough? I don't want a kid, just to have a kid. I'd only want one with you, ever." That "last" tear I thought I'd cried? I hadn't. Davis' sweetness has them rolling down my cheeks again. He keeps going, "I'm okay with no kids as long as I have you – and it would be hard to make out on the floor of the closet if we had kids."

I slap his chest teasingly, my sniffling slowing down. I shake my head in agreement. "We'd have to get a lock on the closet door."

Davis, still holding me, my sobbing over, kisses my forehead, then stares into my eyes and winks, "If we ever get pregnant, I'm calling the locksmith, immediately."

I don't think we'll need to call the locksmith.

Chapter 3-Past: 6 months ago

"I wish I could tell you why you aren't getting pregnant, Biz, but I really don't know," my OB, Dr. Shaner says flatly. "I'm a bit frustrated with your case to be honest. There's really no reason you shouldn't be."

Those are not the words I thought I'd be hearing two and a half years after I first proposed to Davis that we get pregnant.

"You think *you're* frustrated?" I reply purposefully snarkily.

I thought I'd be hearing things along the lines of, "Oh, she is so adorable," and "It looks like she'll be having a little brother or sister soon," from strangers as they met me and looked at my first beautiful child and growing belly holding my second. Evidently, I won't be hearing any of that.

I'm a medical mystery it seems.

Davis and I have both been examined thoroughly, repeatedly. There is nothing wrong with us physically. Davis' sperm count is normal. Thanks to medicine like Clomid and Ovidril I'm ovulating more regularly than my usual super-long cycles that resulted in only five periods a year. I actually thought of that as a blessing until now. Even intrauterine insemination failed. Our doctors can't figure it out, other than to tell us to relax. We've talked about in-vitro and adoption, but neither of us have pushed it past the talking stage. I don't know if we've given up or are refusing to give up. What started as an adventure, an exciting new turn in our relationship, has become a topic of sadness and frustration.

So we are putting it on hold, after almost three years of trying. Being parents isn't completely off the table, but it was starting to put pressure on our marriage. A marriage that started out with lots of challenges. If I'm honest, I have to admit, I won't miss the oral meds and shots. They were making me sort of, well… a bitch. I don't know how Davis survived my mood swings. It was Davis' idea to take a break. We are still young, both under 30. Part of me feels like I've given up… failed. Another part of me is… relieved.

As unsuccessful as we have been in the baby-making arena, even though we've tried (lord knows, we are very good at trying,) Davis and I have both been amazingly successful in our respective careers. In the four years we've been married, Davis has become a well-known set and lighting designer, locally and regionally. It all may blow up big, soon, since he is also the lighting designer for Charlie's band, Boxwood, which is about to go on a national tour opening for the very popular, award-winning band, Lawnmower.

After Neil's trial, I gave the interview I promised Gail, my producer at KTTA. I could never have imagined the response I received afterward. I, suddenly, became the face of victims standing up for their rights, especially victims of sex crimes. We were able to start the foundation I mentioned to Davis right after the trial. When I say we, I mean, Davis and me, with financial assistance from his parents, and Jules, my best friend. Jules runs the Brandon-Connelly Foundation for us. I always knew she was good at organizing and would do something big. She is good, really good. I have never seen anyone with so much natural fundraising acumen. So, Jules runs the foundation and Davis and I give lectures – he about mental illness and families, I about how to avoid becoming a victim of a sexual predator and what to do if you are.

If you had asked me in college what my life was going to be like in the years ahead, I could never have guessed this. I don't do the lectures for a living, only to support the work of the foundation. My real job is still at KTTA, but I'm no longer a production assistant. I'm a producer, well, an associate producer, but still a producer. I'm in charge of the day-to-day on "Happening in the STL," along with my colleague, Henry. Gail has been moved up to executive producer and basically oversees us. I like being a producer. I prefer being behind the scenes, but due to my notoriety, shall we say, because of the Ireland case, I'm occasionally asked to be on-camera or sit on a panel. I'm still not super comfortable getting recognized when Davis and I go out, but I'm almost used to it. The people in this city are pretty respectful to their local public figures and athletes.

So, I'm taking a break from the pursuit of "baby" and focusing on Davis and work… and my godchild, Kitten. Yep, Jules and Charlie have a little girl named Kitten. Kitten Boxwood. Unlike Davis and me, they got pregnant immediately, like on the first try, after deciding. Kitten was born around the time of Davis and my second wedding anniversary, so she'll be three in the fall. I have never been as crazy about any other human being in the world, other than Davis, as I am about Kitten. She's what makes me want to have a baby AND what makes it okay if I don't. I really don't know how Jules does it all, wrangling a rock star husband, a very busy little girl and a foundation all at once. I'm just glad she does.

Chapter 4-Present: Kitten

"Dammit!" I bellow, as a stack of my best dishes crashes to the floor and shatters all over the kitchen.

I hear a small, sing-song-y cherub voice echo me, "Dammit, Dammit, Dammit, Dammit!" I've never heard the word said with so much glee. Frankly, I don't know whether to laugh or cry at this moment. I do both.

In seconds, my best friend, Jules Hagen-Boxwood, is standing at the entrance to the kitchen with a mini version of herself, her daughter Kitten Boxwood, in her arms. Kitten is still singing her "sweet swear word" song. She may look like Jules, but she is Charlie all the way, personality-wise.

"What happened? I thought you were just coming in here to get a drink?" Jules asks, as she toes a couple of shards of dish away to make a path to me. "Are you okay?"

I laugh/sob and look at Kitten. What the hell is wrong with me?

Jules answers her own question, "Oh. Oh no, you're not okay."

Jules hands Kitten off to me and then wraps us both up in a hug. One of her patented "Jules hugs," but with a little less bounce and more care.

Jules takes charge of the situation immediately, "Kitten, you and Aunt Bizzy go into the family room. I'll get this cleaned up."

"K, Mommy." Kitten replies, "Aunt Bizzy, come on." Still in my arms, Kitten points to the family room.

I hold Kitten tightly, give Jules another squeeze and whisper into her ear, "Thank you."

As I move out of the kitchen, carefully dodging the broken crockery, Jules calls out behind me, "I'm coming out there as soon as I clean this up to find out what's going on with you."

Before we even make it to the sofa, Kitten cups my face in both of her pink chubby hands and asks, "Aunt Bizzy, why come you cwyin'? And waughin? You hit youw funny bone?"

"No, baby, Aunt Bizzy is just a little sad, I guess, and then I heard your cute little voice and it made me happy at the same time," I explain.

Kitten looks me straight in the eyes and says, "OK," like what I said makes perfect sense. She kisses me on the nose and then wraps herself around me with her arms and legs, like a pygmy marmoset, and hugs me. She even gives me a few pats when she hears me exhale. So like her mother in that way. In every other way, she is her daddy's girl. I predict Kitten will be front and center singing with Boxwood, or maybe her own band, before we know it.

Jules is at my side in just a few minutes.

"I think you're going to need to go shopping. You took out half of your Kate Spade dinner plates."

I repeat my sentiments from the original incident, "Dammit!"

My echo returns as Kitten again says, "Dammit!"

Jules and I laugh out loud. "Jules, I'm really going to have to watch my language around her."

Jules snorts. "Are you kidding me? She lives with the lead singer of a rock band. I'll be lucky if she doesn't get expelled from preschool."

I'm a bit calmer now, being cuddled by Kitten, Jules holding my hand.

"So, what's going on? Broken dishes, cussing, tears, laughs, you're all over the place today," Jules says gently.

"I really don't know…" I say, but then it all floods out. How I saw Jake and it triggered me thinking about the past few years, the challenges – trying and not getting pregnant, the trial, and the good things – Davis, her, Charlie, the foundation, my great job at the station, and most of all Kitten. I tell her that I know how fortunate I am. I'm a very lucky girl and I don't know why I'm all mixed up emotionally.

"Well, for one thing, you're coming off all of those crazy fertility drugs. And I bet you're about to have your period."

"Yeah, I am," I confess, but I don't think that's all.

Jules probes further, "You haven't said anything about that madman, Randall, still being out there. That's not hitting your radar?"

It isn't. I explain that the police have been vigilant. It appears that Randall has dropped out of sight. Nobody has seen him or reported anyone looking like him since I last saw him under the bridge – years ago, after he nearly killed Davis. Donnie Garrett, the investigating detective, keeps the case open and provides regular updates. He has also become a good friend to us and the Brandon-Connelly foundation. Donnie thinks Randall may be gone for good.

"So, a baby...you *really* want one, huh?"

I sigh and nod. "More than I realized."

Jules is three months pregnant. Kitten hasn't been told yet. Jules and I begin to speak in code.

"Biz, you're okay with this, right?" Jules makes a circular pointing gesture at her belly.

"Oh, my gosh, of course, Jules. Never, ever think I'm not happy about that." I am a bit envious, but I'm completely thrilled that Jules and Charlie are having a second baby. I just wish it was me. "I just want a baby, too." The sobs return.

Kitten sits bolt upright in my lap. I thought she was napping, but I was wrong. She was listening. Kitten brings her tiny hand up to my jaw and turns my face to hers, directing my attention from Jules. Her expression is quite serious.

"Aunt Bizzy, you don't need no other baby...you hab me."

The laugh/crying commences again, and this time Jules joins in. The wisdom of my toddler godchild is great. I kiss her cheek and say, "You know, Kitten, you are probably right."

The front door to the condo bangs open. Charlie and Davis appear. Their hearty chuckles stop suddenly as they witness the huddle of women on the couch, bizarrely laughing and crying.

Kitten hops off my lap and runs to her handsome daddy and uncle in the foyer.

"Daddy!"

Charlie scoops her up. After a quick hug, Kitten reaches out for Davis. Charlie passes her off to him. They both look confused, but pleased at the attention from the little charmer.

"Uncle Day-Bus!" Kitten gives him a big squeeze and plays with his hair, like she always does.

Day-Bus. It's an even better nickname for Davis than "Mavis."

All the grown-ups laugh and repeat Kitten's words. "Uncle Day-Bus." She squirms out of Davis' arms and returns to my lap.

Davis' eyes have been on me since he entered the room. He knows something is off. He follows Kitten over to me on the sofa. He sits on the opposite side from Jules. I'm surrounded by concern. Charlie comes over too. He sits on the coffee table right in front of me. Davis wraps an arm around me and pulls me closer.

"What? What's going on?" he asks.

I open my mouth to speak, but am cut off by a tiny rapid-fire soliloquy.

"Day-Bus, Bizzy bwoke all your dishes. Then she said, Dammit! Then she cwied. Then she waughed. She did not hit herw funny bone. She is happy, but she is sad because she doesn't hab no baby. I told her she didn't need one, 'cause she has me. Oh, and the dwugs make her cwazy." Having synopsized the situation, Kitten jumps off my lap and waddles off to the guest room, where we keep her toys.

Davis, Jules, and Charlie are wide-eyed. I can tell they are restraining themselves from busting out laughing as Kitten leaves.

"Man, we are in trouble," Charlie gets out between snorts, "she's a fifteen year old in a two and a half year old's body."

I say, "I guess she was listening."

Davis looks a bit confused.

I continue, "Well, Kitten pretty much bottom-lined it. I have to clarify, I *accidentally* broke half of our dishes, not ALL. And I am VERY happy with my life. And I am still a little sad, you know, about…"

Davis finishes the sentence, "no baby."

I tilt my head and press my lips together in agreement. "I'm fine, really. We've been through this. At this point, if it happens, it happens. And like

Kitten has reminded me, I have her." I reach over and place my hand on Jules' belly. "And this little guy...or girl."

"Are you sure?" Davis asks with an uncertain tone, "You're not just saying that to gloss over everything? Because I want to know if something's really wrong."

I reassure Davis. And Jules and Charlie. "No, I'm fine...really."

Jules pops up and in typical Jules fashion pronounces that she and I need a Girl's Day Out... or weekend... or vacation. Her reasoning is sound: I'm worn out, she's pregnant and we haven't had a vacation in a long time, either of us. I'm about to protest when I catch Davis and Charlie looking at each other and smiling slyly.

***

"So? Whaddya think?" Charlie says with his eyebrows raised and hands upturned in question.

Jules is bouncing around the family room in celebration.

We quickly discovered what was behind the boys' smirks. My emotional meltdown couldn't have come at a more opportune time for their proposition. Boxwood is going on a big tour, the biggest of their career thus far, in the summer. The rehearsals and the technical rehearsals with the sets and lights are starting in a little over a week in Atlanta. Charlie was *going* to propose we all go down together during the rehearsal period, since Davis needs to go too, to do the lighting design. Jules' declaration gave him another idea. He and Davis will go to Atlanta. Jules and I will go to a resort in Florida and get pampered. While I'm a little leery about being away from Davis, it sounds delicious. Sun, warm water, sleep, quiet time, and girly stuff, like shopping and manicures.

"You girls need to relax..." Charlie says smoothly. "We're going to need you all rested up for visiting us on tour this summer." Aaaahhh, the ulterior motive comes out. Jules smacks Charlie on the arm.

Davis is still at my side on the sofa. He's moved me closer, wrapping me up in his arms. He rubs the tip of his nose against my ear and whisper-growls, "Yeah, Rest up." Sheesh, that is hot!

Jules and I agree to the plan. We are chattering wildly about where we will go and what we will do…or not do, like maybe we'll just veg in our bikinis all day, when something strikes me.

"What about Kitten?" I ask.

Davis and Jules say, "Oh." I think they actually may have forgotten she factors into the plan, they were so caught up in the idea.

Charlie puts up a hand and waves it back and forth quickly to indicate, 'No problem.' "Already taken care of. When I hatched the original plan, I made a call to Jules' parents. Grandma and Grandpa Hagen are ready to take delivery of our small, blonde wiggly package whenever we're ready."

I need to get a bikini.

Chapter 5-Present: Packing

We're going on vacation! Well, Jules and I are going on vacation. For twelve days. To a beautiful resort on the white sands of the Florida panhandle. Right after Charlie proposed the idea and we agreed, Jules went on the internet and found the most amazing, secluded 5-Star condo resort. Evidently, it's where all the "beautiful people" stay when they are there. It's out on a peninsula, away from the really touristy part. I called Gail and was, thankfully, able to arrange some vacation time on short notice. I don't have any on-air commitments in the next 3 weeks and Henry can take over anything that's in production, along with the assistants. I just need to go in and get everything set up for them, so it runs smoothly. And there is always the cell phone in an emergency, but I'm not sure Jules will be thrilled if that happens. And the best part, Davis and Charlie are going to join us at the end for three or four days. Second honeymoon. Davis and I leave tomorrow for our respective destinations. I've been packing all afternoon.

"What are you doing in there? How's it going? Are you organizing my socks again?" Davis shouts to me.

"Noooo," I reply from the walk-in closet. I'm gathering more things to pack for the trip, and trying on my new bikini. I rearrange the bottoms a bit, pick up my beach bag and step out of the closet to show off my swimwear. Davis turns to look at me and I whip off a model turn, throwing the bag over my shoulder with a flourish.

"Whoa, you're *not* wearing that." Davis states. I've never heard him tell me I can or cannot wear something. He must be joking.

Laughing it off I tell Davis, "Of course, I am. I got it for Florida. I'm just showing it to you."

"Uhm, no you're not. All those damn spring breakers down there this time of year? No, not wearing that." Davis is quite insistent.

"There won't be that many spring breakers. It's almost the end of spring break. They certainly won't be looking at me, I'm an old lady."

Davis is shaking his head, "Yeah, right. Old lady. You're 27 and really hot." He's now moved over to me, taken the beach bag out of my hand and tossed it onto the bed by my suitcase. Davis snakes an index finger under one of the strings holding up my bikini top and slides his finger up and down. I can't say I don't like it.

"It really is a great idea – the vacation. I think it might be just what I need." I say. Davis frowns. I hope he doesn't think being away from him is just what I need. That's not what I meant.

I'm just about to open my mouth to tell him so, when he says, "I know it's a great idea. I just wish I had thought of it before Charlie. I'm kicking myself. I had a feeling you were a little blue. I just wasn't intuitive enough to think of it before he did. I'm sort of pissed with myself."

It doesn't matter who thought of the idea. I certainly wasn't thinking of a vacation, prior to Jules mentioning it and Charlie running with it. "It's okay, baby. Mavis, I didn't even see the need myself."

Davis has slipped his fingers up both strings of my bikini top, all the way behind my neck. He's working at untying the bow holding the top on. "Yeah, well, from now on, I'm going to be … Much. More. Attentive."

Davis is slowly untying the lower set of strings of my bikini top, while holding the top ones. Once I feel the final loop slip, he flings off my top, so I am standing, in only my bikini bottoms, my breasts lightly grazing his t-shirted chest. His fingers are skimming ever so delicately over my shoulders, arms, across my chest, until I believe they have reached their chosen destination. Davis teases my breasts and nipples with light, stimulating touches. It's different and making me oh-so-excited.

"What are you doing?" I tease, lifting my eyes from watching his hands to make eye contact. I notice the green of his eyes is now almost forest, his pupils large and black.

"I'm helping you pack your swimsuit."

"Oh, well, you missed some of it." I slide my hands lightly down his chest and abdomen and when I get low enough, point with one finger to my bottoms.

Davis leans in and whispers hotly, "Don't worry. I'll get to that." He reaches out and takes both my arms, puts one on each of his shoulders, and in one smooth move, grabs me around the waist with one arm and hikes me up onto his waist. I automatically wrap my legs tightly around his hips. His face is eye level with my breasts and he takes full advantage of the position. His free hand cups and manipulates my breast as his thumb strokes the nipple roughly. It quickly tightens into a deliciously painful point and just as quickly is covered by Davis' punishing lips. I arch slightly, thrusting my core into his now hardened crotch, building the excitement below and causing a tugging tension where his lips are on me, circling and sucking. I'm so caught up, I don't really notice we've moved, or Davis has, until I feel myself being lowered and see suitcases and clothes and accessories flying off the side of our bed.

"So much for packing," Davis growls.

He lifts me up on the bed, so my head practically hits the headboard. I reach down and grab the bottom of his t-shirt, pulling it frantically over his head and throwing it heaven knows where. I have a brief, hilarious thought of what our bedroom must look like right now – the antithesis of "packed and ready" for sure, well maybe just the antithesis of "packed," because we both are definitely ready. I move quickly to remove Davis' shorts, pushing him to the side of me to get a better hold on his zipper. He has managed, while I was focused on undressing him, to untie my bikini bottoms, pull them out from under me and chuck them into the sea of unpacked vacation wear. He barely kicks off his shorts when one and then two of his long, strong fingers breech my folds and are in me, stroking my g-spot in a "come to me" motion. He presses his thumb onto my clit and circles slowly. The two contrasting motions have me swirling and bucking in response. I groan and it is at once silenced by Davis' lips coming down on mine. His tongue pushes into my mouth and begins the same circling and stroking his fingers are so deftly engaged in. I can barely think, my hands are one minute clutching his back, then his hair and they finally slam back onto the bed as I grasp at the duvet. The ascent is so measured and powerful. I kiss Davis back, trying to keep up stroke for stroke. I am dangerously close. I want him in me. Reaching down, I grasp Davis' cock. It is hard and pulsing, but almost silky to the touch. I circle the crest of it with my own thumb and suck on Davis's lips and tongue, as if I were down there. He moans loudly when I do.

"Put your hands up on the headboard and hold tight," Davis commands. I do.

He pulls away from me, rears back on his knees, lifts my hips up and slams his hardness into my wet, wet folds.

I hear myself moan with pleasure and relief, "Aaaaaaah!" as Davis does the same. Holding firmly onto the headboard, my ass in the air, I meet Davis with each stroke as he pounds into me, holding me to him with one strong, straining arm.

The movement is at first slow, deep, heavy and then increases to a pounding staccato.

Davis' gaze is boring into me, "Don't let go of the headboard." He pulls my pelvis toward him, seating himself even deeper, one arm still encircling me, one directing the movement of my hips. I am almost completely off the bed, with the exception of my shoulder blades. I don't know how much longer I can hold on, to the headboard, or to delaying my pleasure.

Davis pulls me toward him with a large tug, while delivering one final deep thrust to my vibrating core. "Uh, Damn. Lizzz-eeerd." I come in waves with him and the deep, throaty intoning of my nickname.

As he pulls out, I sigh, "Oh, Uh, Wow. Just, Davis, Wow."

"I know," Davis says, still panting. "And that's just packing. Imagine if we took a real vacation."

"I'd never see the pool or the beach, would I?" I ask, jokingly.

"Nope, and come to think of it, I'd be a good way to keep college guys on spring break from ogling you. I may have to put off Atlanta and go with you." He's laughing, but there is a tinge of seriousness to his words.

I roll over so I'm half on top of him, throw one leg across his hips, grind a bit and then rain kisses on his chest. "It's supposed to be a 'Girl's Only' thing, Davis. You and I will have some time at the end."

"Okay..." Davis concedes with a fake pout. "But I did just demonstrate the effect of that bikini on a dude, so keep covered up, okay?"

I agree, to prevent any further discussion, "Fine, I'll wear a sarong."

"Not much better... hmmm, I'm going to be thinking about getting that bikini off you again the entire time I'm away from you."

I confess, "Good. That was my plan."

I pick my head up from his chest and look around our bedroom. It looks like a Target store blew up. Turning back to Davis, I shake my head while resting it on his chest and tell him, "You are terrible at packing."

"What?" He responds slyly, "I thought that was great packing. If you like my packing, you should see how I unpack."

I'm looking forward to coming home as much as leaving now.

***

Charlie and Davis toss our bags up onto the conveyor belt outside Security. Davis adds a dramatic grunt, "Uhh. What did you put in there, Lizard? Depleted uranium?"

When he turns back around to make a goofy face at me, I smack his upper chest scoldingly, "No, just shoes and swimsuits and stuff."

"Whose shoes? Frankenstein's?" Davis teases me more.

"No. I just don't know what I'll need. I want to be prepared. And it's *not* that heavy. You lifted it before."

The four of us walk to Security. Charlie and Jules are in front of us, their heads close together, whispering and sharing small intimate kisses on the cheek and nose as they go. Davis and I hold hands. He does my favorite thing – rubs his thumb across my knuckles. Mmmm – Davis' thumbs. They might be one of his best body parts. At least in the top five.

When we arrive at security and our departure is imminent, I'm suddenly a little anxious. I haven't felt this way in a long time. My panic attacks have been under control for years, thanks to Dr. Matt and all my compensatory strategies. I've just not been away from Davis for any extended length of time since we got married. A day or two, now and then, but never this many nights in a row. It's something we agreed to without words after being apart for three months before we got married. We've always managed a way to work our schedules so we aren't apart. I suddenly miss Davis, even though he's right in front of me.

Obviously sensing my unease, Davis says, "Hey, You okay?"

I nod my head, fearful that if I talk I'll cry. And there really is no reason to cry.

As if reading my mind he tells me, "I'll miss you, too. It's only nine days. You'll have a good time." Trying to make me laugh, he adds, "I had a really good time 'packing' last night." It works. I smile broadly and am rewarded with Davis' smirky smile and naughty eyebrow raise.

All I can say is, "Packing," as I recall the fun of last night. I tuck myself further into Davis' embrace and pop up on my toes to give him a slow, deep kiss. He moans his approval of the move.

"Davis, say it!" I demand.

"I love you," he replies quickly.

"And I love you, too. But that's not what I want to hear." It's my turn to raise my eyebrows and tilt my head.

Davis hums and taps his temple with one of his long fingers, "I don't know if I can say it and mean it."

"Please… it's so reassuring when you say it. Like my day can't start without it."

Davis concedes. I can see Jules out of the corner of my eye, signaling that we have to get going through Security.

I push further into the embrace, pleading physically.

"Oh, okay… HAVE FUN!" Davis finally spits out.

I kiss him one more time and tell him thank you and I will.

I turn away from him, immediately missing his warmth. Getting into the Security line, I purposefully don't look back at him, when I hear in a whisper-shout, "But not too much."

I lift my head and turn from reaching for a plastic tub. The only thing I see in the sea of people is Davis' face, his lips puckering into an air kiss, a devious wink of one emerald eye and his huge smile. I can just make out him mouthing, "Love you," when the TSA agent yells for me to keep moving and Jules tugs on my jacket, bringing me back on task. I proceed through the Security line, turning back quickly to try and get one last glimpse of Davis. When I do he's gone. I think, "Love you, too, Day-Bus" (giggling internally at Kitten's nickname for him). I know we'll probably text each other throughout the week, so I'm not really sad. I'm just always better with him around.

Chapter 6-Present: Vacation

"Shut your mouth."

I look at Jules incredulously and reply, "I didn't say anything."

"I know you didn't. Your mouth is hanging open."

And well it should. Jules and I are in the back of a taxi, having just been driven through the gates to our incredibly luxurious and exclusive resort. I realize that my mouth is, indeed, agape. I take Jules' words to heart, close my mouth and gulp. This place is gorgeous, and HUGE. From the taxi, I view an expansive pool area, with what appears to be a zero-entry, sand-bottomed infinity pool. It looks like the pool goes on forever, as you can't tell where the edge of it is and where the ocean begins from this perspective. The pool area is all done in whites and soft pinks. Towels are laid over the back of each inviting lounge chair. The blue of the pool is like none I've ever seen before, the same color as the Gulf of Mexico. Yes, this will do nicely for twelve days. If I'm this impressed with the pool, I wonder what the condo and beach will be like?

The taxi drops us at the lobby, I pay and tip the driver after he hands our luggage out to us. He thanks us and then gives me a card with the taxi information, "in case we want to leave the resort for dinner or dancing or something." Right now, I see no reason to leave at all, but I take the card, just in case. I pull up the handle of my suitcase and roll it into the lobby. It's exquisite – beachy, but elegant. It's slightly odd to see people in swimsuits and sandals milling about in a lobby with pink marble tiling, pillars and a chandelier. It's a very different feel from the chilly Midwest we just left. Tugging on my suitcase and viewing the attire of those around us,

I realize I've brought *way* too many clothes. I could probably survive with two or three swimsuits, a couple of sundresses, t-shirts and shorts.

Jules goes to the desk and returns with two key cards.

"We have a Gulf view on the tenth floor. I booked us into a condo with two master bedrooms, both with views," Jules tells me excitedly. She is practically bounding through the lobby as we walk to the elevators.

"If I haven't thanked you yet – Thank. You," I say sincerely. Jules, the master organizer, has thought of everything. I haven't done anything to help with the planning of this trip, except purchase resort wear and pack (with help from Davis. Oh, boy, did I pack!).

Once in the elevator, Jules presses the number 10 and then turns and wraps me up in a giant hug.

"No thanks are necessary. You know I love planning stuff. Thanks for letting me take care of it all. I think it will be a good break for us both."

I'm curious, so I ask, "Won't you miss Kitten?"

"Yes, I'll miss her every day, but I'm also looking forward to sleeping in, reading an entire magazine and not having a chaperone for all bathroom activities." Jules sighs happily at the prospect.

"I guess that means we have separate bathrooms?" I tease.

"Absolutely. It will be nice to have some space to myself. At least until Charlie gets here." Pointing to her belly, she adds, "This may be my last chance before the next one comes."

Jules doesn't look pregnant. I can tell she's pregnant, because, well, she's my best friend, but to the rest of the world, she looks like a hot chick with big boobs – boobs courtesy of the pregnancy. According to Jules, it's Charlie's favorite part of pregnancy. That and the second trimester horniness.

"God, I'm so glad I'm finally past the first trimester. I was nauseous until a week ago. I finally feel good," Jules tells me. Charlie should be a very happy man when he gets here.

Surprisingly, I'm not sad or envious when Jules talks about being pregnant. It's the next best thing to it happening to me, because she shares every horrible, disgusting and wonderful part of it with me – including the baby at the end. One thing we absolutely share right now is fatigue. We are both exhausted from the trip.

As we unpack, I yell to Jules' bedroom, "I think we need to go to the store and stock up for the week."

"Ugh, I'm tired," Jules shouts back, "Can't we go later?"

I wander into the condo's gourmet kitchen to get a glass of water and see that it is already full of all our favorite foods.

"Jules, I don't think we have to go. Come look."

Jules, now barefoot and in a loose sundress, comes into the kitchen. She looks around and jumps up and down, clapping her hands. "They thought of everything, didn't they? Coffee, soda, chocolate, yummy bread, cheese, even gummy bears." We examine all the cabinets and the fridge. We are set. Charlie and Davis took great care of us.

"You do look a little tired, Jules. Why don't you have a nap and when you wake up, I'll make dinner and we can eat it out on the balcony. We can make our plans for the week," I suggest.

Jules sighs and nods her head, "That sounds like heaven. I'm going to open the sliding door in my bedroom so I can hear the ocean."

I walk the few steps toward her and give her a squeeze, "Excellent idea. I'll wake you for dinner."

I go to my bedroom and open my own sliding door leading to the balcony. I step out and look out over the ocean. The sound, the smell, it all relaxes. I close my eyes and enjoy the warm breeze blowing across my skin. I have an idea, walk back into my room, retrieve my phone and return to the balcony. I take a picture of the view and text it to Davis along with a message:

> We are here. It's beautiful. Thanks for doing the grocery shopping. Tell Charlie Thanks too. This is the view. I can't wait to share it with you. <3 Biz

I wait a few minutes. Davis doesn't text back. I look at the time on the phone. I realize he is probably still on the plane or just getting off in Atlanta. Their flight left a few hours after ours.

I'm feeling a little wiped out myself, so I set the alarm on my phone for an hour, lie down on top of the king-sized bed and look out at the blue, blue ocean sky. Just a little nap, that's all I need.

***

"Biz?"

Davis turns to me and shakes my arm. I wake up and see we're in the waiting room of an airport. I'm confused. What am I doing in a waiting room? In an airport? How did I get here? I'm on vacation with Jules.

"Don't worry. We'll catch the next one. We'll get home to the kids. Don't worry," Davis rubs my arm some more.

The kids?

I look down at Davis' hand on my arm, it changes to a woman's hand and then I hear, "Biz?" again. It's a woman's voice. It's Jules'. I look up from the hand and see my best friend cuddled up next to me.

I blink repeatedly and then stare up at her. The light in the room has dimmed. It's a diffuse pinky-orange. I look all around and come to the conclusion that the airport waiting room was just a dream. I think it was a good dream. I was waiting for something. A plane. I was going to "take off," to my – kids. I smile up at Jules. "I just had the nicest, weirdest dream. It was short, but it made me feel happy."

Jules pushes a bit of hair out of my face, just like a mom would do and asks, "What was it about?"

I tell her about my brief dream. Davis, me, waiting to get on a plane to go to our kids.

"Have you ever had a dream come true, Biz?"

I think back to when I first met Davis. I had a dream he came to me, began to make love to me. He was wearing a black shirt and had cut his hair. Months later, when we did get together, he was wearing the exact shirt and had cut his hair. I smile to myself before I answer, "Yes, I have. I married him."

"Maybe this one will come true, too."

That would be nice, I think to myself. I wonder if it means we'll be flying somewhere to get our children. Adoption?

Jules pulls back the covers and changes the subject, "Now, get up! It's time for dinner." Jules moves off the bed and goes to stand in the doorway of the balcony.

I sit up and stretch. "*I* was going to make dinner."

"You were sound asleep and I woke up early from my nap. You slept right through your alarm. Guess which one of us was more tired?" Jules winks at me. "I made shrimp risotto. The guys thought of *eve-ry-thing*. They even had whoever brought the food in write down a few meal suggestions."

Still in my t-shirt and boxers, I join Jules in the doorway. The sun setting over the Gulf of Mexico, stretched out in front of us, is glorious. Now I know where the light in my room came from. I inhale. The clean, salty, slightly water-heavy air refreshes me. Looking out over the balcony, I see families launching kites into the wind. Little children squealing with laughter as they catch the sea breeze. Fathers' deep chuckles. I can smell steaks grilling in the pavilion below. Mothers setting tables with picnic ware. I didn't realize I was so tense, until just this moment, when I consciously feel my shoulders relax.

"Let's have dinner out here. On the balcony," I suggest, not looking at Jules, but continuing to take in the sights and smells of my temporary resort home.

"My thoughts, exactly," Jules agrees.

We set the table with the nautical-themed dishware and light a few candles in metal lanterns and bring them out to the table on the balcony. Jules and I eat a leisurely dinner of risotto, salad and for dessert, key lime gelato. I thought briefly about having a glass of wine or beer. Being pregnant, Jules can't drink and I'm not super interested in drinking alone. Instead, we both succumb to that delicious southern drink – Sweet Tea. We discuss our plans for the week and agree that nothing should feel like work. So, lying on the beach, reading, swimming, lying by the pool, shopping, going to the spa, eating, drinking more sweet tea (we clink our wine glasses full of it together), watching movies and lying around the condo – that's the agreed-upon plan. Lots of lying around. We begin to discuss the next day when both our phones alert in chorus. Jules and I look at each other and shrug.

"Really?" Jules giggles.

We pick up our phones, show the names on the screen to each other and say our husband's names out loud.

We both shake our heads. Jules snarks, "Checking up on us already."

I open Davis' text fully.

> Hi, Lizard Baby. We're in Atlanta. That's a beautiful view. Can't wait to see it with you. Going to bed-big day tomorrow and for the next few days. Will fall asleep looking at a better view-a picture of you. Love you.

Davis really likes pictures. He's a pretty visual person.

I text back.

> Love you too. So much. Remind me to tell you about my dream.

My phone alerts again as I'm about to put it down.

> I will. HAVE FUN.

I smile to myself and clutch my iPhone to my chest, as if it were a conduit to Davis' arms. I look across the table. Jules is texting and mumbling and softly laughing to herself. I go back to my dinner.

I hear Jules set her phone back on the table. "So they're there. What did Davis say?"

"Just that he was going to bed and he couldn't wait to see the view here. I sent him a picture earlier. How about Charlie?" I ask.

"About the same. And then he sent me a few selfies that Kitten took on my mom's phone. Look." Jules holds up her phone for me to see a picture of Kitten wearing a tiara and making a duck face, just like a teenager.

I sigh and say, "I love that kid."

"She loves you."

Finishing our meal, we finalize tomorrow's plans while cleaning up.

Chapter 7-Present: The Beach

We hit the beach early. Rambling across the wooden bridge that leads over the dunes to the beach, I scan the horizon and then pull my view back, widening it. I see we practically have the whole private beach to ourselves this morning. There are a few runners and the beach crew setting up the chairs and umbrellas. There are, actually, more gulls and shore birds than people. The tide is out and the birds are finding their breakfast in the sand.

"Good morning, ladies!" a slightly rough-edged voice pulls my attention from the peaceful beach. A very handsome guy, like VERY handsome, is looking up at us from the end of the wooden bridge. Ridiculously tan, spiky, sun-bleached blonde hair and muscles visible, even through the clothes on the few parts of his body that are covered. He's wearing colorful jams and a faded blue, worn t-shirt with the arms cut off. The word RENTAL is stretched across the front in large white block letters.

Jules turns her head, widens her eyes and whispers what I'm thinking, "We can rent *THAT*?" and then she whistles lightly.

We both giggle like tweens.

Rental boy interrupts, "I'm Crush."

Of course his name is Crush. Why wouldn't it be? Hot beach boy wearing a RENTAL sign t-shirt named Crush. Of course that's who two married women would run into the minute they hit the beach. As we move closer, I realize he's not so much a boy as a man. From the crinkles around his eyes as he smiles up at us, I gather that he's actually older than we are, maybe early thirties, but with a phenomenal body. I don't feel so bad about ogling him now.

42

"I'm your rental guy." A million inappropriate responses enter my brain. I just hope I don't verbalize any of them and embarrass myself. "What can I get for you ladies? Chairs? Umbrella?"

Crush explains to us that we can rent the lounge chairs and umbrellas by the day or the week. One of the beach crew will set them up every morning by eight o'clock and put them away at four o'clock in the afternoon. They are ours all day. We'll know how to find them in the morning, because there will be a sign with Jules' last name on the back of the chairs. Jules takes over and makes all the arrangements with Crush, while I stand and well, basically, gawk. Crush directs us to a pair of lounge chairs and an umbrella that are already set up.

"Just let me know if you need anything else, okay, ladies? If you need the umbrella moved or you want to go kayaking or out on the catamaran. I can hook you up," Crush says before turning to leave and help the other guys. I'm sure he's being so attentive because we're the only ones on the beach. What a nice guy.

"Oh, my god. Everything that came out of that guy's mouth sounded dirty to me," Jules says, "Am I right? Or is it just my pregnancy hormones firing out of control?"

I laugh out loud, "No, I was thinking the same thing. He was so hot. At first I thought he was just a kid, but once we got closer…"

Jules starts organizing our beach area, but looks up to waggle her eyebrows at me. Grabbing my elbow, she whispers loudly, "I know!"

Jules and I spend the morning on the beach. It begins to fill up with college kids and families on spring break by ten. We get about two hours of quiet to read and lounge until the noise of the other tourists begins to penetrate our peace. The tide has come up. It's the perfect time to go for a swim.

The rising tide provides us with killer waves on which to body surf. We laugh and tumble, the motion pushing us out of control like toddlers. Upon exiting the ocean, we are exhausted and happy, laughing at the top of our lungs.

As we pack up our beach bags to go in for lunch, our boy (we've decided he is "our" beach boy), Crush appears.

"You ladies going in for a while?" he asks.

I giggle, like seriously giggle and widen my eyes at Jules, keeping my face turned away from Crush. "Uhm, Yeah, Crush…we're gonna go have lunch. It's getting kind of crowded out here."

Crush replies, "Between ten and two are the busiest time. All the college kids. They don't wake up early. I prefer the early morning." Crush looks out at the water. "Most mornings the dolphins are out there jumping. Maybe you'll see it. Morning, man. It's just so sweet."

The intonation of his last phrase instantly brings to mind Jeff Spicoli, the surfer stoner from *Fast Times at Ridgemont High*. Looking over Crush again, I can see a resemblance – tan, sun-bleached blonde hair, crazily white teeth. Yup, Spicoli, all grown up and with a job.

We are halfway across the wooden bridge spanning the dunes when we encounter three, obviously college age, guys. I'm only twenty-seven, but I'm surprised by how young they seem. Young and carefree.

If it is, indeed, possible to be eye-fucked, Jules and I were getting eye-gang-banged. The three cuties, (yes, it's true, way cute), gave us both the once over as we passed them on the bridge.

"Wait! Where you going?" one of them said.

Are they talking to us?

I turn, push my sunglasses down my nose to peek over them, and with the same hand point to myself.

"Us?" I ask.

"Yeah," another one of the guys says. "You abandoning us when we just got here? It's not fair."

We laugh out loud, wave them off and keep walking toward the condo.

The first guy calls out after us, "No, really, where ya goin'? You look so fine this morning. Don't deprive us."

I think I have giggled more this morning than I have in years. I've also not had this much obvious attention from any man other than my husband in a while. It's weird and flattering. It feels good to be silly.

The guys don't stop. They have continued to yell to us. "Don't leave." "Come to the pool tonight." And my favorite, just because it made Jules squeel and grab my arm in disbelief, "Shit, did you see that blonde?... Holy fuck!... she was so HOT!"

***

We're going to the pool tonight. Not because the Spring Break guys invited us there, but because tonight we've decided to cook out. The resort has a large pavilion with gas grills, available for any of the guests to use. It's adjacent to the pool, so you can cook, drink, look at the view and take a dip in the pool if you get too warm.

Steaks, grilled corn and sliced tomatoes are on the menu for tonight – one of my favorite summertime meals. I'm in charge of the grilling. Jules is sipping on a travel cup full of sweet tea and lounging in the sand at the shallow end of the pool, singing along to the music that's playing on the speakers. I think the song is, "Like a G6." Pool music. She looks over to smile and make a face at me while I cook. Just as I call to her that our dinner is ready and begin to take the steaks off the grill, I notice that she has been joined by two of the Spring Break guys from the bridge this morning.

"Okay, guys, I gotta go. You heard the lady. Dinnertime!" Jules informs them.

One of them looks up toward me and gives me an up-nod. Then I realize he's responding to the guy at the grill beside me. College guy number three. I didn't even know he was there. He was so quiet and I was busy grilling and watching Jules. He seems less rowdy than the other two. Light brown hair that's cut in a short, preppy style. Behind his hipster glasses, he has some of the darkest brown eyes I've ever seen. He's about Davis' height, but with a narrower frame.

"Looks like it's our dinnertime, too," I hear the guy that looked up, say to his friend and Jules.

The larger of the guys walking over with Jules says, "Let's all eat together."

Before I can open my mouth, Jules responds, "Sure."

It will be a table for five in the pavilion tonight.

I introduce myself to Spring Break guy number three, the cook, "Hey, I'm Biz. Looks like we're having dinner together."

He lowers his head, smiles shyly, and steps toward me. I notice he wipes his hand on his baggy cargo shorts before offering it to me to shake it. He makes eye contact briefly, only once our hands touch, and says, "Nice to meet you. My name is Quarter."

I've never heard anyone with that name before. "Quarter? Is that a family name?" I ask.

Jules and the other boys have made their way to our table at the pavilion. Jules is grabbing plates, cups and silverware from our basket and starting to set the table.

One of Quarter's friends, the one with a blonde buzz cut and matching tribal tattoos around his biceps, answers my question, "'Quarter' is short for Herbert Edward Dow, *the fourth*."

Quarter concurs, almost embarrassed, "Yeah, I'm a fourth. And Quarter is better than being called Herbie."

I have to agree and nod while looking at him with a smile on my face.

Jules introduces herself to Quarter, then tells me the other two guys' names, Jack, the one with the buzz cut, and Clay. They both reach across the table to shake my hand. Clay is the beefiest of the three. He's wearing a backward baseball cap, reflective aviators and has a full arm sleeve tattoo with images of pin-up girls and classic cars. Oh, did I mention none of them is wearing a shirt? None of them.

As we eat and share all of our collective food, we find out the guys are from University of Georgia. Clay proudly turns his ball cap around to show me the logo and the mascot, UGA the bulldog, emblazoned on it. They're all juniors. Quarter is majoring in engineering, Jack in education and Clay has been taking biology and chemistry in hopes of getting into vet school. It's funny, they look like "party boys," but each of them is rather passionate about what they're studying.

"Where do you ladies go to school?" Clay asks. It may be one of the most flattering questions I've been asked in a long time. They've got to be messing with us, because we are both wearing our wedding and engagement rings.

"C'mon, seriously, you guys know we're old married ladies, don't you?" Jules laughs and holds up her hand.

Jack blurts out, "Nope, don't believe it. You can't be more than twenty-two or twenty-three, tops."

The whole table is laughing now.

"Cute, very cute. We've been out of school for a while." I assure them.

"And married?" Clay asks. "Wow, lucky guys." He looks around curiously, "Where are they?"

Jules fills them in on Charlie and Davis' whereabouts, "My husband is a musician and her husband..." she points to me with her pretty pink manicured pinky, while holding an ear of corn, "is the lighting designer for the group. They're rehearsing in Atlanta. They'll be down at the end of the week."

Quarter, who has barely said a word, other than to explain his name says, "Boxwood."

Clay and Jack's heads pivot to look at him, like he just said something inappropriate or crazy. Jules and I join in staring at him. How did he know?

"Uh, yeah..." Jules stutters, "How did you know?"

Quiet Quarter suddenly becomes quite animated and sputters out, "Your chairs on the beach say, BOXWOOD, and I thought to myself when I saw it, 'Oh, like the band.' And then you said your husband was a musician. Is your husband Charlie Boxwood?"

I ask, tentatively, "You guys know who Boxwood is?"

They all nod vigorously and say, "Yeah." "Sure." And "Yeah, they play them on the college station in Athens all the time. Most college kids know Boxwood. They're awesome." Clay, Jack and Quarter begin rattling off the names of Boxwood songs. Songs we are very familiar with. It's surreal.

Jules and I look at each other astounded. Boxwood is bigger than we thought. Jules promises to introduce them to Charlie when he arrives. They are well and truly excited about the prospect.

After we finish our long, fun dinner, we load our supplies into a beach bag and move to head upstairs. The guys ask where we're going and we tell them we're going to watch a movie and then go to bed. They complain that it's too early for the night to end, but I'm able to distract them by pointing out three young ladies having cocktails in the pool.

"Quarter?"

"Yes, Miss Biz," he drawls.

"You see those beautiful girls over there?" I ask.

He lowers his head, but raises his eyes to look at them. "Yeah, I see'em…"

"Well, the one with the long wavy black hair has had her eyes on you all during dinner. I suggest you go introduce yourself." This boy needs a little push, I can tell.

Quarter shakes his head back and forth, silently refuting my statement.

I have an idea. "Jack, Clay…Please, help this boy out and walk him over to those pretty girls and make him introduce himself. I think it could work out well for all of you."

"Oh, yeah…" The boys have finally noticed the college girls. Clay and Jack punch Quarter on the shoulder and "assist" him to stand. "We're on it, Biz," they tell me.

I can just make out the sound of the guys saying "Hi" to the college girls and them giggling in response, as Jules and I exit the pool area. I'll just add matchmaker to my list of skills.

"Hey, Jules, Biz," Clay hollers out to us, "Remember, we're going to The Snapper some time this week. All of us."

Jules and I widen our eyes and both say, "YESSSS!" in an exaggerated fashion. Over dinner, the guys made us promise to go out dancing with them one night at a local nightclub, The Lucky Snapper. I guess being closely linked to Boxwood increased our cool factor even further with them.

Jules and I are going to have a great time giving each other shit for hanging out with Spring Breakers, even after we assured our husbands we wouldn't.

Chapter 8-Present: The Lucky Snapper

The next six days are unhurried and restful. I've barely thought of any of the things that have been stressing me out – primarily, the infertility. We exert ourselves only to go to the beach and prepare food. One of our afternoons is spent at a large outlet mall. We return with bags of cute outfits for ourselves and Kitten. I splurge on four, yes, four pairs of shoes-Louboutins, Manolos, Jimmy Choos, and a pair of Yves St. Laurent sandals with metal ankle straps. I've been coveting them since I saw them in last September's issue of Vogue.

I even bought something for myself at the Agent Provocateur outlet store. It's a black bra with crisscrossing bondage-type straps and matching panties and a garter with the same crisscrossing. It has a name. Whitney. My lingerie has a name! Not the kind of thing I've ever bought before. Jules gave me the nudge I needed to go through with the purchase. It actually may be more of a present for Davis than for me. I'm not sure when I'll spring it on him.

I hide the Agent Provocateur bag in one of the bigger bags. Since we've been here in Florida a strange thing has been happening. Evidently a good portion of St. Louisians like to vacation here. It's the closest beach to our town, twelve hours away. I've been spotted several times as "that girl, Biz, from 'Happening in the STL'." I'm glad it's not, "that girl, Biz from the sexual assault trial." I've only done the occasional broadcast, on "Happening," but I guess it's enough to be mildly well known. I make sure to always be friendly. St. Louis is a large city with a small town gossip grapevine, but I hide the Agent Provocateur bag because, hey, they don't need to know what kind of lingerie I'm wearing. After I'm recognized a few times, I begin to observe more and more Cardinals ball caps and Missouri license plates. It *is* a small world.

Another afternoon we indulge in the full spa experience – manis, pedis, massages, wraps, scrubs and Vichy showers. I have never been so polished or had such hydrated skin ever. It's probably a good thing too, after being in the heat and sun for several days.

Walking out of the spa, Jules wonders aloud, "How am I ever going to go back to the Foundation and work all day after this vacation?"

"I know," I agree, "I wonder if I'll even remember what KTTA looks like." It's strange. I've missed work, but not enough to call in or check my email.

"Well, I'm going to enjoy it while it lasts. I've been answering emails…"Jules says. I shoot her a disapproving look, "…and I've got a lot of work to do when we get back."

"Why, what's up?" I ask.

"You're kidding, right?" Jules admonishes, "The Ball? The Brandon-Connelly NEVER AGAIN Fundraiser. Did you forget? It's five days after we get home."

I had.

I confess, "Actually, yeah, I did. I have my dress and everything. I guess, I'm just so relaxed here, it slipped my mind."

My stress level is way down from where it was seven days ago. And Davis will be here in two days. I can't wait to see him. He may never get to the beach, I miss him so much. He's going to be attacked by a plumper, pampered, chilled out Biz.

Getting back to the condo, we see Clay, Jack, Quarter and their "new" girl friends, heading to the pool. Quarter spots us getting out of the car and diverts himself to meet us.

"Hey, we're going to The Snap tonight. You coming?" he asks eagerly.

Jules and I look at each other and both shake our heads no at the same time.

"Thanks for asking, Quarter, but we're all relaxed from our spa day. I think we're just going to order a pizza, flop out on the sectional and watch chick flicks."

"No. I mean, you promised" Quarter protests. "And we only have a couple more nights."

I speak up, "Tomorrow."

Jules looks at me with surprise. "You don't want to wait until Charlie and Davis get here to go out dancing?"

I tilt my head and raise an eyebrow at Jules. She should know that after this many days without Davis, the last thing I'll want to do is take him out dancing with strangers.

"Oh, right!" Jules finally clues in. "Yeah, tomorrow, Quarter. We promise." We both cross our hearts and hold our palms up to swear to it.

***

We meet our three "dates" for our night of dancing at the pavilion. They all look so handsome and young. They've gone all out. No backward ball caps or baggy shorts.

Crisp button-ups, tight jeans (smile) and styled hair. I notice they are alone, none of the girls that have been hanging around are with them.

"Where are the girls?" I ask.

"What girls?" Clay answers with a smirk.

I make a bug-eyed smarty pants face at him. "The girls you've been hanging out with," and then add with a whisper to Jules, "and making out with."

Jules giggles.

"I think you two are all the 'girls' we can handle tonight," Jack tells us, turning on the charm.

"Two to Three, huh?" I tease.

Quarter has been quiet this whole time, but softly interjects, "I think you can manage it."

Jack and Clay punch him on the bicep and ruffle his hair, both teasing and praising him for his newfound smart aleckiness.

I agree with Quarter and tell him so, "I think you're right, Quarter. Let's go dance."

We take two cars. The five of us won't fit in the sports car Charlie and Davis rented and had waiting as a surprise for us at the condo. Clay comes with me. Jack and Quarter take Jules in their big red pick-up with a lift kit. I can hear her say, "Cool truck," as they hike her up to help her in.

***

The Lucky Snapper is a family restaurant by day, a large open air bar and dance club by night. It's located right at the entrance to the bay that connects the Gulf of Mexico and the Intercoastal Waterway on a marina. Lots of patrons simply dock their boats and climb the steps to the club for the evening. The theme of the club is, of course, fish and fishing, but with disco lights. It's perfect for the area. Even if you were to come to The Snap in the winter, it would feel like summer. Tonight, since it's the weekend, there will be fireworks at midnight.

The club is already rocking when we arrive. Locals and tourists mingle. You can tell the difference. The tourists look a little more cleaned up, like they would back in their cities and hometowns when they go out. The locals are dressed like the tourists do at the beach – shorts, tees, sundresses over bikinis. The guys grab up a tall table, somehow, and hold out the chairs for us. Jules orders a soft drink. The guys get a bucket of beer and I decide to join them in the local favorite. The beer is ice cold and goes down so easily. I have to remind myself to slow down. Clay, Jack, and Quarter are complete gentleman and take turns dancing with Jules and me. They never leave one of us alone or even look at any of the other girls in the club. And there are plenty of cute ones checking them out. They must be wondering what three college guys are doing with two almost-30 year olds.

After a few dances with Quarter, he guides me back to the table. Jules is already there. I am SO thirsty. I start in on my second beer and decide I have to ask what I've been wondering "Quarter, why are you guys out with us tonight? Why are you being so nice to us?"

"Yeah, Why?" Jules joins in the questioning, "Why aren't you out with your hot babes?"

Clay snorts and tells Jules, "You're a hot babe. You're Charlie Boxwood's hot babe. You said you'd introduce us. We just want you to have a good opinion of us, so you will. Introduce us."

Jules laughs out loud, "So you're flirting with me to get to my husband? That's a good one." She dramatically sighs and laughs again, "At least you're honest."

Jack stops Jules' fake mini pity party. "Oh, don't be deceived. We totally would have fired on you both. Hard. But then you said you were married and that…that's just not cool. And well, fuck, sorry, you're Boxwood's babes."

Jules' and I laugh 'til we cry, "Boxwood's babes! Charlie would freaking love that!" The funny thing is, it's actually true.

As we laugh and talk, the words to the song the DJ is playing hit my cerebral cortex and the lyrics register.

"Southside girls can always get dates.

All the streets are named after states.

Looking for my beauty queen

My southside, southside Miss America dream."

I look at Jules, Jules looks at me, we both turn to the guys and then all of us scream in unison at the top of our lungs, "BOXWOOD!!"

Oh My God, I've never heard Boxwood in a bar before. I mean, I have, *LIVE*, but not being played by a DJ. We abandon the table and rush to the dance floor to rip it up to "Southside Miss America." I'm impressed to see that Clay, Jack and Quarter know all the words.

The song is about the part of our town where all the streets have the names of states. It's also a lower socio-economic area with rapidly changing areas of diversity. Boxwood wrote the song with the idea that they could change the street names in the song by wherever they are playing at the time. It's sort of genius. On this version, the recorded one, they end with the girl being a "Show Me" girl from Missouri Street. Jules is dancing and smiling and singing – LOUDLY.

She yells out, "That's my husband!"

The whole bar is singing the song. How did we not know everyone knew this song?

***

We learn pretty quickly from other bar patrons that "Southside Miss America" is in the Top 100 for Pop/Rock. Charlie never called to tell us and oddly, we haven't been listening to the radio much. I'm so excited for Charlie and the other Boxwood guys, Simon, Ian and Colin. There are no harder working musicians and they've certainly paid their dues over the past four years. Jules asks the DJ to play it again after a few more songs. She videos the bar crowd all singing along and dancing and texts it to Charlie, squealing the entire time.

There is a 99.99 percent chance we are closing The Lucky Snapper down tonight/this morning. I've danced almost continuously since the first time they played Boxwood's hit. Boxwood's hit! When I do take a break, I quickly down more beers with the guys. I'm buzzed, but not too badly. Just crazy relaxed and happy. The only thing that could make it better would be Davis – here.

After the fireworks, they announce last call at the bar. Jules has rushed off to use the bathroom before we leave, claiming she'll never make it home if she doesn't. I wonder after she slips away if I shouldn't join her. I've had a lot of beer.

After I throw in some cash, and argue with Clay about doing so, he pays the tab. Glancing up from putting my wallet back in my crossbody bag, I look across the bar and spy Jules talking to a guy in a Cards ball cap. He's turned three quarters of the way away from me and I can just barely see his profile. I think he looks familiar. He has hair the color of Davis' and the same length too. I know it's not Davis because this guy is shorter. Jules is nodding and smiling. She points over her shoulder at me and the guy quickly turns his head to look in my direction for a second. I feel myself inhale sharply. It can't be! It can't be him!

The guy turns away and I see Jules mouth the words, 'Bye,' as he leaves. The lights in the club come up fully and everyone still in the place moans and shields their eyes. The bartender claps his hands three times loudly and proclaims, "People – Closing Time. You don't have to go home ... but you can't stay here." This only causes the remaining crowd to begin singing the Semisonic song that states the same sentiment. It doesn't get them moving any faster. I don't join them in moving, or singing. I'm frozen. I just keep looking at the place where the guy in the baseball cap was talking to Jules. Even as she comes toward me, my focus is still behind her.

"Hey, Biz ... I just met another one of your fans..." Jules announces.

I shake my head no. And then say it. "No."

"What do you mean 'no'? The guy said he recognized you from your show. He's originally from St. Louis, moved down here a few years ago...and you know what's weird, it just hit me...that guy had a shirt on that was just like the one Davis used to have. Did you ever see that old shirt that Davis had that said, 'An Awkward Morning Beats A Boring Night?' Biz? Biz?"

Jules' words are swirling around me. She shakes my arm violently. It's as if I've been smacked in the forehead by a two by four. A guy, that looks like Randall is wearing a shirt that looks like one of Davis'? It *was* Randall! I'm sure of it. Where did he get that shirt? I've never seen one like it before I saw Davis' and I threw that one in the trash. Could he have gone through our trash, back home? Surely not...

I ask carefully, "Jules, the guy. Did he say his name?"

"No, we only exchanged a few words," Jules' forehead is pinched and furrowed, "Why?"

"It was Randall." I state without emotion. I can't have any emotion. I'm not letting myself, because I don't know which one will overtake me right now. Or maybe I'm just in shock.

"What? No. No, that wasnnnt... Oh my god! That *was* Randall!" Jules is shrieking. I am silent. "He looked different. I mean, I've never met him, but he didn't look like the pictures I've seen. Biz, Jesus! What are you gonna do?"

What am I going to do? What *am* I going to do? I let the emotions come. First, I start shaking, then I think I'm about to cry, but I don't. I count and exhale. It all turns and I grit my teeth together, swallow hard and let the anger come. No more crying. I AM NOT going to panic. This is the moment when I could easily spiral down, fall apart. Suddenly, with laser-like focus, I know what I have to do. I say, mostly to myself, "ENOUGH!" I turn to Jules, Clay, Jack and Quarter and tell them purposefully, "Come on. We're leaving. Now! I have to make a phone call." I know precisely to whom I need to talk.

***

I go in a completely new and liberating direction with my plan of action. When pushed, human nature dictates – people will first act the way you expect – then if pushed further they will zigzag off course and do something completely out of character.

My first response, so far in my life, to an emotionally challenging event, is to cry and run away. But not this time. This time I'm zigzagging. This time I'm not waiting for anyone to tell me what to do. I'm not going to try to hatch a plan in isolation. No. This time I'm calling in back-up. I'm rallying my troops to make sure Randall Ireland never hurts any girl again.

I explained the Randall situation to Clay on the way back to the condo. I have Jules, Jack and Quarter on speakerphone on my cell, so they can hear, too. The boys are livid. They can't believe, as they say, "that fucker has gotten away with this." Jules and I decide we will go straight up to the condo, just to be safe. Clay volunteers to walk us up, but then insists that he and the other guys hang out downstairs by the pool and in the lobby to make sure nobody has followed us. And they want to call the police. I encourage them all to hold off until I can make a phone call.

Chapter 9-Present: Vacation's Over

I don't call Davis.

I don't call Dr. Matt.

"Hell … (yawn)o," a sleepy female voice answers the phone, surprising me. Crap! It's three o'clock in the morning. I'm so wrapped up in what I want and need to do, I didn't even think before I dialed his number.

I reply, "Hello, Um, Hi, This is Biz Connelly-Brandon. I was, umm, looking for Donovan Garrett, Detective Garrett…"

The woman on the end suddenly becomes very serious, "Yes, sure…Biz, hi, this is Posey. Posey Garrett. I'm Donnie's wife. We met at a charity event one time." Then I hear her whisper, "Donnie, babe, wake up." Then a little louder, "DON-O-VAN, Wake up! It's Biz Connelly." She returns to talking to me, "Biz, he's coming to the phone. He was out late on a case." I can hear unintelligible words and grumbling in the background.

The voice on the other end of the phone changes to a deeper, gravely one, "Biz, what's up? It's three-o-five in the fucking morning. This better be good."

"Donnie, he's here." It's all I need to say.

"Randall Ireland?" Donnie asks for confirmation, vocal roughness gone.

I note how calm and even my response is.

"Yes. Randall Ireland is here."

***

"Okay, bye. Two days. My condo," I finish my lengthy call with Donnie, throw my phone across the bed, burying it in the pillows and lean forward, covering my face with both hands. I don't know if I'm praying or begging. I just hope this plan works.

There is a soft 'click.' I pull my hands away from my face, look at the carpet and slide my eyes across the floor to where the 'click' came from – the door.

At the end of my visual trek, I'm met with a pair of bare feet. A pair of bare feet I know and love well. I can't believe those feet are here. I follow the feet up to the face I also know and love well. Davis. He's early. I didn't expect him until tomorrow, which, technically, it is.

Davis tilts his head, pushes his lips into a tight line and surveys me with his breathtaking green eyes. Even with concern in them, they are devastating. Without words, he's asking me how I am. It's amazing, but those zaps and buzzes I felt early in our relationship whenever I saw him, overtake me now, filling my chest with anticipation. I feel my heart pumping wildly. Relief and excitement twirl around into a tornado of emotion. I push my hands down on either side of me and launch myself off the edge of the bed, flying into Davis' arms.

I slam into Davis, pushing him up against the door behind him. I can't get close enough as I crush him, throwing my arms around his neck and grasping his hair with my fingers.

"Hey, Hey, baby. Lizard, baby… Jules told me. You saw Randall" Davis says, comfortingly. I'm not crying, but my relief can't be held back. I let out a long cleansing sigh and melt into Davis. He rubs my back with his thumbs until my breathing becomes more controlled. Finally, he pulls me back slightly, pressing our foreheads together and asks, "How are you?"

How am I?

I'm scared. I'm (slightly) anxious and panicky. I'm angry… really angry, but after talking to Donnie and now, being in Davis' arms, I'm EMPOWERED.

I don't answer with words. I lightly kiss Davis. It's all I want right now. I've missed him so much. More than I realized. Our kisses escalate, longer, slower until I beg with my tongue for him to open his mouth. Davis willingly accepts the offer and soon our lips and tongues are sliding and sucking deeply at each other. Our kisses become crushing and full of painful passion. I just want to feel him and from his response he does, too. I reach around behind Davis and turn the lock on the bedroom door.

Davis reacts to my unspoken direction in a snap and wraps his arms tightly around my waist, lifting me so my feet are just off the floor. I'm fused against the entire length of his body. I can feel his erection against my lower abdomen. Davis must be able to feel my sharpened nipples through my shirt, as well as the heat that must be meeting his erection below.

As he walks us back across the room to the bed Davis asks hotly, "Are you sure? You don't want to talk? You're okay?"

"No talking. Not now. I just need to be with you. I need to feel strong," I reply as he lies me down across the width of the king-sized bed. Davis and I waste no time. I rip open his button snap short sleeve denim shirt and rake it over his shoulders and off of him. I want to feel him, naked, against me. Now. Davis' hands reach down for the hem of my sundress and in one adept move, remove it up and over my head. As my hands fumble to get rid of his khaki cargo shorts, Davis' lips are all over my face, his strong, capable hands cradling my head. They don't stay there long before he moves them down to cup my breasts, dragging his roughened thumbs over my achy nipples. I arch into him, while my hand slips into his boxer briefs to stroke his throbbing, ready to engage cock. I hum with happiness. Fuck everything negative. I'm taking control of my life. I push the plans made with Donovan out of my thoughts and focus fully on taking control of Davis.

Once I've rid Davis of all his clothes, I become even more assertive. I roll, so Davis is now beneath me. Crawling downward, beginning at his collarbone, I kiss across and down his firm, muscled chest. I breathe in his warm, spicy, slightly sweaty scent and blow my hot breath down, down over the hills of abs until I reach my destination.

Feeling Davis' hardness in my mouth, I'm quickly over the edge. My hands slide slowly across his hips, my thumbs at the place where the muscular "V" ends. My core is flaming, slick, needy. Davis intuitively knows and as I lick, swirl and plunge my mouth onto him, he reaches down and after deftly making my panties disappear, slides a long finger into me. His thumb presses and strokes my now blossoming clit. I plunge once more down to take Davis as far as I can into my mouth without gagging. I pull up to attend to the warm crest of his cock, swirling my tongue around it several times, before powering into the notch with extreme suction. Davis moans loudly. His fingers and thumbs stop moving. I can feel he is getting close and I want him in me when he comes. I want to be drowning in his green eyes and screaming his name.

I release Davis' cock from my lips after a few more deep kisses. Davis is sprawled across the bed panting. He reaches up to hold my hips, his large hands cupping my ass, to guide me onto him. He pushes up and in as I grind my vibrating core down to make the exquisite connection. Straddling Davis, I take him into me. I contract around him and after I feel him fully seated within me, my body spontaneously clenches and releases. I groan with pleasure and relief. Davis continues to guide my hips, rocking and thrusting. He slips one hand forward and again finds my clit. Again, he presses, releases, circles, presses, releases.

My build up is becoming evident. I lick at the fine sheen of sweat accumulating on my upper lip, then I bite my lower to hold the sensation back until it's time to let it go. Davis' other hand goes to one of my breasts, his fingers extending and stretching my nipple. I could come with just that slightly painful move. I arch into his hands, both upper and lower, supporting myself with my hands behind me on Davis' thighs. Davis' hands, thumbs, cock are hitting all the right places. Suddenly, Davis sits up and sucks my breast into his mouth licking and sucking violently, both his hands go back to my ass, bringing us impossibly close together. He thrusts deeply and powerfully. I stop breathing for a moment and let go, coming for him. I scream Davis' name… "DAY-A-VUS!!"

Everything goes fuzzy, then black.

***

My vision returns after a few moments and as Davis pulls out I collapse next to and partially on top of him on the bed.

"Mav… I think I passed out for a few seconds. Did I pass out?" I ask.

Davis chuckles and pulls me even more on top of him, "You're eyes were sort of far away and then they rolled back. I'm guessing that felt pretty good, huh?"

"Amazing, powerful, just what I've been missing and needing," I answer.

"Yeah, you 'Googled' me pretty damn good, Lizard. I may need to go away more often," Davis says with mock seriousness.

I freeze.

Davis senses my tension, "What?"

"No, thank you," I tell him sincerely, meeting his eyes dead on.

The truth is, after my discussion with Donnie, Davis may need to "go away." I drop my gaze and then my head to the space between his jaw and shoulder. I sigh and breathe him in.

So missed.

It's time. I need to tell him the plan Donnie and I have come up with. And I need his blessing to make it happen.

I lift my head a tiny bit and kiss Davis jaw right below the ear, enjoying the roughness of his scruffiness. I formulate the words to start this most difficult of conversations, when there is a percussive assault on my ears. It sounds like a million fists are pounding at the door to the bedroom.

"Biz, Davis, get up, open up… something's happened" Jules is yelling through the door frantically.

The rapid knocking doesn't let up. Now, Charlie's voice joins Jules', "Davis, man, let us in. NOW!" I've never heard him sound so very concerned. There's a darkness in Charlie's voice that's scaring me.

Davis looks up at me, his eyes wide, brow furrowed and slides me gently to the side of him. He's up and pulling his jeans over his nakedness in seconds. He snatches his t-shirt from the bedroom floor and as I sit up, he throws it to me, indicating I should put it on. Davis marches toward the door. I fumble around in the sheets, retrieve my panties and slide them up my legs and into position just as he opens the door.

Charlie and Jules are standing in the threshold, both of them with their hands covered in blood.

I hear screaming and painful moans from behind them.

I rush up to join Davis and can see where the noise is coming from behind my bloody friends.

Jules shrieks out, "It's Quarter! Randall attacked him!"

Davis and I must both be is shock, because we just stare at one another for a moment open mouthed.

Davis asks to no one and everyone, "Who's Quarter?" He gets no reply.

Again, I feel the storm of emotions I did at The Lucky Snapper, but with more rapidity. Panic. Here, then gone. Fear. Again, only for a moment. Anger. HERE. Present. Now unabated.

Darkly, I voice what everyone already knows, "He's here." Meaning Randall.

All present silently acknowledge with nods of their head. I know they are all waiting for me to freak out, but I'm not. While I *am* scared, I know that Randall trying to get to me means he is desperate. He's right in the headspace where Donnie and I need him to be. I smile.

Jules says something so uncharacteristic of her, "Why the fuck are you smiling, Biz? That lunatic is here. On the resort grounds. Only moments ago he was just a few floors away."

"I'm smiling because Randall has tipped his hand. It's just as Dr. Matt and Donnie suspected. He's stalking me." Charlie, Davis and Jules all gasp audibly. I push through them and see Quarter sprawled on one of the couches of the sectional. His face is smeared with blood and one of his eyes is swelling visibly with each passing moment. His face looks different, broken. Clay and Jack are pacing around him, firing a million questions at him. Thank God someone thought to recline him on the couch and give him a cold washcloth. Quarter pats at his face with a shaky hand. I sprint over to him and sit in the small open space by his side, facing him. Taking the washcloth from his hand, I slowly, carefully wipe away the blood. I can sense everyone else in the room huddling around us.

I speak quietly, my voice strangely tiny, "Quarter, oh my God, what happened?"

"I was out by the pool gate, thinking everything had calmed down. You know, we were back at the resort and your husbands had arrived." Quarter, even bloodied and beaten, politely looks at Charlie and Davis and stammers, "Hi, Gu – guys, nice to meet you."

Davis comes up and puts one hand on my shoulder and reaches out to shake Quarter's hand with the other, "Nice to meet you, Quarter."

Jules and Charlie move to stand by Jack and Clay at the back of the couch. Charlie reaches over and shakes Quarter's hand, too. He tells him, "Man, we're so glad you, all of you..." Charlie up-nods to Clay and Jack, "were here to look out for our girls. What happened next?"

Quarter takes a deep breath, "Like I said, I was standing by the pool gate. Jack and Clay were walking around the resort, sort of doing one last check to see that there wasn't anyone around. I was about to go upstairs to our condo when I spotted, through the lobby windows, this guy with a green shirt and a baseball cap on backward, hanging around the elevators. I thought it was weird, like why would you pace in front of the elevators, why wouldn't you just stick in your key card and call it. Then I realized, the guy didn't have an access card. Cardinals Hat, Green Shirt. He was THE Guy. The guy bothering Biz. The guy from The Snap that she told us hurt her. I didn't really think, I just went over and asked if I could help him. Get a better look at him.

"He was really worked up and he said he left his key upstairs and he needed an access card. When I said no... it all happened so fast, like out of the blue, he punched me in the eye. It shocked me. He started to lurch for my pocket, like to get the access card, and I went at him with an upper cut. I think that's when he punched me in the nose..." Quarter reaches up to gingerly touch his nose and winces. It strikes me, *that's* what I perceived as different when I first saw him lying on the couch. His nose is visibly broken – turning at an almost 45-degree angle to the right.

Jack and Clay take over the story from Quarter. They saw the fight. They saw a commotion in the lobby through the window from across the parking lot. They started running toward the lobby and yelling. The ruckus alarmed Randall because the guys report that right after he punched Quarter, breaking his nose and knocking him out, Randall looked out the window, made eye contact with Clay and ran. Jack ran after him, but Randall must have hidden or found some way to escape because Jack lost him in the under-building garage full of cars. Jack and Clay brought Quarter right up to our condo.

Clay pronounces, "We gotta call the cops!"

I look at Quarter, then Davis and finally everyone else in the room. I return my attention to Quarter, "Thank you for stopping him…"

Quarter opens his lips, the ones still smeared with blood from his broken nose, "But I didn't…"

"No, you did. You stopped him from getting to me tonight. Can you do something else for me?" I question Quarter sincerely, "Can you put off calling the cops?"

Quarter looks at me for what feels like a full minute, never breaking eye contact, "Sure, Ms. Biz… whatever you need."

His friends protest loudly and with a lot of profanity, "Quarter, what the fuck, man?" "We need to crush that guy!"

I say calmly but not loudly, "Quiet." The guys continue their rejection of my idea to leave the cops out of this.

"Quiet!" Quarter yells at them, stopping the din immediately. His hand goes back up to his face, like it hurt to be that loud. "Let Biz talk," he adds.

I explain to all of them, Davis, Jules, Charlie, Quarter and the guys, that I need to leave Florida immediately.

"I need to get out of here and get home to St. Louis. If we call the cops here, they'll keep me here. Donovan…" I touch Davis' hand and pull him toward me to look deeply in his eyes, "you know Donovan, Detective Garrett? Well, he has an idea. A way to apprehend Randall. It depends on me getting home and Randall hopefully following us there."

Davis shakes his head. I can't tell if he's disagreeing or merely trying to comprehend what is happening.

Quarter agrees not to call the cops. I insist he go to the hospital. His eye and nose are starting to look really bad. The upper half of his face is really swollen. Quarter has agreed to tell everyone he ran into one of the poles in the garage. It's a plausible story for his injuries. The plan is to call an ambulance. The commotion of it arriving and taking Quarter away will make a perfect cover for Davis and me to get away. While everyone at the resort is watching the ambulance, Charlie and Jules will "sneak" us out to the airport. Our "sneaking" will only look that way to everyone *not* monitoring my every move. Meaning to everyone, except Randall Ireland. We are going to "sneak" out to make sure he sees us.

After it's all settled and before the ambulance is called, I leave the group and fly back into my bedroom of the condo to pack as quickly as possible. Davis' bag is still packed from his trip down from Atlanta. He follows me into the bedroom, pulling his cell phone from his back pocket.

He begins a conversation with I don't know who, "Hey, man. Yeah, yeah, it was really great to get here so fast. Thanks again for the lift. Uh… could I ask you a favor, like a huge one…" Who the hell is Davis talking to? "I need to get my wife out of town quickly. She, uh, we think she has a stalker… Yeah, I know. Crazy. Yeah, that's what I was going to ask. I owe you, huge. Thanks. Okay, we will. Bye."

I'm baffled by Davis' phone conversation. "Who were you talking to?" I ask.

"Matt. He's the lead singer of Lawnmower. I didn't get a chance to tell you he gave us a ride down here to Destin on the band's private jet. He was feeling like a little time off himself. He's gonna let us borrow the jet to get home."

I'm momentarily speechless. Boxwood *is* on the rise, if Davis is talking to the lead singer of one of the hottest bands in the country and has his number in his contacts. When I finally regain control of my speaking abilities, I blurt out, "Wait, Matt?… You mean, Matt Chambers… of Lawnmower? THE band, Lawnmower… gave you a ride and is letting you… us… use his plane?"

Davis smiles, his patented, symmetrical dazzling smile and tells me, "Mmm…Finally. The chatter. I almost wish we didn't have to leave." Davis walks over to me, pulls me into his arms and kisses me soundly. I wish we didn't have to leave either. Then he collects himself and answers my question, "Yeah, he's a good guy, all of the Lawnmower guys are. Are you almost ready?"

"Almost," I answer. "Go tell Jules to call the ambulance."

Chapter 10-Present: Run Away, Baby

The sun is up. And I have not slept all night. Most of the not sleeping was great. The Snapper. Dancing. Hearing Boxwood's song in public. Davis. Nearly-sent-into-a-coma-sex. The rest of the not sleeping, well… it was a nightmare. A fully conscious nightmare.

The paramedics have arrived and are strapping Quarter to the gurney. He's answering questions, but he looks drawn and exhausted. Pain can do that. We all follow the paramedics and him down to the ambulance. Davis carries both of our suitcases. My hand is grasping his upper arm. I'm so tired, but I keep pushing back against it. It's not the time to fall apart or fall down. I can do that after we are away from here.

Clay goes in the ambulance with Quarter to the hospital. Jack plans to follow in the truck. They've promised to send me text updates about how Quarter is doing. Charlie is going to swing by the hospital later and make sure all of Quarter's bills are paid. I made him promise.

In a spectacular show of lights and sirens, the ambulance delivers an early morning wake up call to all of the tourists in the condos. Jules tells me some of them are out on their balconies watching the hubbub. I've stayed "hidden" in plain sight in the lobby. Charlie goes and gets our rental car and pulls it up to the lobby entrance. We make a scene of looking out the door and around the under-building garage. Then Davis and I run to the car. I jump in the closer side. Davis chucks our bags in the trunk and runs around to the other side and gets in. Jules rides shotgun.

I don't know if Randall is out there spying, watching my every move. I only hope, now, that he is. He's managed to do it for the past few years and stay off the radar. But his slip up at the bar just "pinged" that radar.

Donovan told me he suspects Randall will now follow me even more closely. It's a game to him. A challenge. I think Donovan's game is better. And Randall watching me now is part of it.

Jules and Charlie are staying a few more days. If Randall hasn't watched me leave, he'll soon figure out I'm gone if Charlie and Jules are here alone.

"Jules, thanks for the great vacation," I say as I hug and kiss my best friend goodbye.

"It was pretty great… relaxing," she laughs into my ear. "Up until that last part… Shit got crazy."

"Yeah, crazy," I agree.

I wonder what she'll think of what's coming next.

Right before we get on Lawnmower's private plane at the small local airport, I text Donnie Garrett:

Getting on the plane to STL. Will text when we land.

Donnie's reply is rapid:

I'll head to your condo as soon as I get your text.

Looks like we're wasting no time with Operation Trap Ireland.

***

Once on the plane, seated and holding Davis' hand, I can breathe again and I exhale. A huge exhale. Davis kisses my forehead and rubs my knuckles with his thumbs. Each move designed to relax me. I, uncharacteristically, order a glass of white wine from Lawnmower's private flight attendant, take three large cooling sips and pass out on Davis' shoulder.

Chapter 11-Present: Home, Sweet, Home

"Hey, we've landed," Davis whispers in a scratchy voice into the top of my head. I remember drinking my wine and then putting my head on his shoulder. Evidently, I was so exhausted I missed the entire flight back.

"We're here already?" I ask and then yawn. I smack my lips and tongue a bit. Ugh! Dry mouth from airplane air. My breath must be delightful! Davis unfastens my seatbelt and I reach down to grab my purse from the floor.

Davis rubs an infinity pattern on my back as I bend and tells me, "I was going to lie you down on the other couch you were so conked out, but I've missed having you near me. You didn't move a muscle once your head hit my shoulder. You were so still, the only reason I knew you were still breathing was your hamster snore. God Damn, it's adorable."

I'm still not really awake, but Davis' hand massaging my back is helping, maybe a little too much. We're still taxiing in. I suddenly realize I probably missed my chance to join the Mile High Club. I mean, how often will I get a chance to be alone with Davis on a private plane? I turn suddenly and launch myself at Davis, pushing him all the way down on the soft, buttery leather couch of the plane. I thrust my hands in his hair and attack his lips. Davis meets my every move with enthusiasm, a lot of enthusiasm from the feeling I'm feeling underneath me!

"What's all this about?" Davis laughs in my mouth.

Pushing up on his chest so I can look down into his darkly lashed green, green eyes I whisper shyly, "I think I deprived you of a golden opportunity by falling asleep on this flight."

"What?" Davis looks at me quizzically. I thrust and rotate my pelvis into his growing hardness. "Oh? You mean, getting my…"

I finish his sentence, "…your Mile High Club card. Yeah. I screwed that up, huh?"

"I'm not too worried," Davis says nonchalantly, "I think we'll have plenty of opportunities in the future."

What in the world is he talking about? We are NEVER going to get another chance to fly in a private plane. We don't know anyone with a private plane. Well, now he knows the Lawnmower guys, but other than that…

I hear the curtain from the other part of the plane being opened and someone clearing their throat. "Uh-hem. Mr. and Mrs. Brandon, we've landed at Spirit airport. You are welcome to deplane whenever you'd like." It's the cabin attendant.

Davis just smiles at her over my shoulder, as I drop my head to his chest, embarrassed at being caught making out. "Thank you, we'll be right out."

Davis slides me off of him and we sit, side by side on the couch. He laughs out loud.

"Busted! I thought we might get initiated after all," he says.

I chirp, "We aren't a mile high anymore."

Looking down at his pants, he draws my attention there, "One of us is."

I shake my head and then squeeze his knee.

Davis stands up, pulls me up off the couch into his embrace and smacks me on the ass. "Let's go home."

***

As we step off the elevator, Donnie Garrett greets us with a wave from our front door. I don't know how he knew exactly what time we'd get here, but here he is. I didn't text him when we landed, only when we took off.

"Why is he here?" Davis whispers down to me. He's squeezing my hand and I can sense the tenseness in his grip.

I squeeze back, more gently, trying to calm him. I whisper back, "I told you. Donnie and I have a plan. A way to stop Randall."

Davis sighs, but continues to walk down the hall. He hasn't looked at me since he spotted Donnie. "I thought coming home and keeping you safe was the plan. Tell me that's the plan."

I reply, tentatively, "It's the first part of the plan."

Davis growls his next words, "I can tell I'm not going to like this plan."

When we arrive at our door from a walk down the hall that felt eternal, Davis snaps out a terse greeting to Detective Garrett. I get the sense he's recalling the deal I made with the STL Metro police to aid with the arrest of Randall Ireland a few years ago.

Davis greets the detective with a surly tone, "Donnie."

"Davis," Donnie responds, then, glances at me, "Hey, Biz." I can see a bit of tension in his eyes. I know he's also not thrilled about this plan, but we need to do it. I need to do it.

Davis opens the door, but before any of us go through he turns and asks Donnie, "Can you... just give us two minutes before we do this? We just got home. We've barely seen each other for almost two weeks and Biz is really tired. Just... two minutes."

Donnie holds up both his hands, "No problem, man. Completely understand. Take your time." Donnie goes right into security mode. He turns his back on us, squares his feet and places his hands behind his back. I see his eyes shift up and down the hall.

***

"Do we have to do this now? Right now? I was hoping to at least have tonight with you." Davis drops our bags in the entry and paces in front of the couch.

I go to him and stop his pacing. I run my hands up and down his arms, trying to soothe. He finally looks me in the eyes. His are damp and glistening. I don't have a drop of moisture in mine. "Hey, Davis... Mav... We *are* going to have tonight. It's going to be fine. Just... please just listen to our idea."

Davis runs his hands through his hair. That's it. That's the motion that tells me he's not okay. He's worried. I reach up and bring his hands down to rest on my hips. I replace his hands in his hair with my own. I could stroke his dark silky hair endlessly.

"I don't want you in any danger, okay?" Davis' voice is rough.

"Okay. I don't think I will be."

Davis cuts me off, "Not, 'I don't think…' NO! DANGER!"

I shake my head yes and then no, responding silently that there will be no danger. I do it, but I don't know if it's true. "We need to let Donnie in. It's been over two minutes."

Davis takes a hand from my hip and waves it toward the door. He motions with resignation.

***

I open our front door. Not only is Donnie there, but Jake is in the hallway. Jake Gianni is standing outside the door to the home I share with Davis. I'm astounded. Jake is the last person I would expect to be here. I turn my head to Donnie. I know my eyebrows must be pinched together and I tilt my head and then shake it ever so slightly, a non-verbal, "What the hell?" shooting straight at him.

I snap my head back to Jake, "What are you doing here?" Before he can answer, I'm right back on Donnie rapidly asking, "What is he doing here?"

Davis calls, "Biz, what's all the noise? What's going on?"

I feel Davis step up behind me and put a hand on my lower back, "Hey, Liz…ar…" He doesn't even finish my nickname, when he sees Jake standing next to Donnie. Davis is not so subdued in his questioning of the situation. "What THE FUCK? Jake Gianni?"

Donnie in a serious tone and measured rate, devoid of emotion tells Davis, "You need to let us in."

If there isn't a linear mark permanently worn into the carpet behind the couch, I'll be amazed. Davis has not been able to keep his seat or his cool throughout the discussion with Donnie and Jake. He's sat for approximately 30 seconds at a time, hopping up and pacing as every new aspect of the plan to snare Randall is revealed. He's sure to have taken the nap on the carpet down by at least half an inch with his constant back and forth. The final step in the plan is divulged and Davis is livid.

"NO! Do you hear me Biz! NO! We will not do this! YOU will not do this! This is… This is fucking insane… No." The last couple times I've seen Davis like this someone got punched or almost punched.

"Jake, Donnie… could we? Could Davis and I have a few minutes?" I ask sweetly. It's up to me now. If we are going to make this plan believable, it's up to me to sell it. Davis won't listen to anyone else. I need to talk to him alone.

Jake takes the hint immediately. Donnie, though an investigator, isn't picking up on the cue that I need to speak with Davis alone to get agreement from him. Jake places a hand on the detective's shoulder, "Let's go down to Starbucks and get a coffee."

A look of revelation comes of over Donnie Garrett's face, "Oh…" He looks at me, I smile tightly and cock my head quickly toward the front door. "Oh, yeah…I do need a little caffeine. Didn't sleep much. Back in say, five…Biz?"

"Make it fifteen." I tell them both.

While I've been "kicking" Jake and Donnie out, Davis has continued to pace and grumble. Once I hear the front door to our condo close, I go to him. I stop his pacing by standing directly in his path, sliding my hands up his chest, over his shoulder and into his hair. I do that thing I like so much. I rub his hair together between my fingers. It's a small thing that can both calm and excite me. Right now, I need to calm. Davis *and* myself.

"Please come sit down with me," I request. "Davis, I can't think with you pacing and growling. I need you to listen to me."

Davis allows me to take his hand and bring him around to the front of the couch. I sit and then pull him down to sit next to me. Usually, after being away from home and each other, this is the moment I'd kick off my shoes, tuck my feet under myself and snuggle right into his side. But right now, I need him to listen to me.

I start to speak, but Davis cuts me off, "Biz... I don't like it. It's risky... dangerous. I think it's dangerous. I am NOT okay with this. How are you okay with this?... with this plan?"

Taking a deep cleansing exhalation, I empty my lungs to release the built up tension. All those years of practicing breathing to allay my anxiety has paid off. When I feel my lungs fill again with new, fresh air, I begin, "I'm okay with this because I don't see another way. I don't want Randall around me. I don't want him stalking me. I don't want him hurting another girl... ever again. I'm not scared, Davis. For once in my life, I am not petrified. I... we can do this. Donnie. Jake. Me. But I can't do it without you. I need you...all in." The only thing I've ever been this sure of before in my life is that I love Davis. I've tried to fix my problems on my own in the past. It worked – partially. Not really. Now I need support. A team. Team Biz.

Davis drops his head and shakes it back and forth, then clutches my hands. "Biz, I'm scared," he whispers roughly. Davis stares at my hands, not me. Then he runs his thumbs over my knuckles. It never fails. It sends a zap straight to my heart and lower. All that caring. All his love. In a tiny glide of his thumbs.

"What part?" I ask, trying to make my voice lower, less excited.

Davis' head tilts to the right and he raises it slightly to look at me with a frown.

I ask again, "What part of the plan makes you scared?"

"All of it. No, that's not true. I'm fine with the first part. The first week, when you're protected and I'm with you... it's the next part. The part when I'm gone."

I look straight into Davis' darkly guy-linered green eyes. The eyes I'm in love with. The eyes that look so torn right now. I tell him, "I don't like that part either. I don't even want to imagine it... but...you do know why this is so important to me, don't you?"

"Yes, I do." Davis tries to smile, but only succeeds in pulling the corners of his lips up from a frown to a tension-filled line, "I think catching Randall, seeing him put away, will give you peace. I feel like just knowing it's a possibility, knowing that you have the power, not him, has already changed you. You know, you seem more in control of this than I am."

"I think you're right, Mavis."

"Mavis…" Davis, finally makes a noise that is positive, a chuckle. "I love when you call me that." Davis pauses briefly and then says quietly, but firmly, "Okay."

"Okay? Like, you're in?"

"I'm in. I'm not thrilled. I'm in no way thrilled. But I'm in." Finally Davis agrees.

I throw myself at Davis, knocking him back on the couch and cover his lips with mine. "Thank you."

Davis pulls me in for a longer kiss, but then suddenly breaks it off, "Call Donnie and Gianni back, NOW. Jesus, I can't believe Jake Gianni is back in our lives. Let's get this thing settled, so I can have you all to myself for one more night."

I practically sprint off the couch and run to my phone to call them back.

***

Donovan's plan to lure Randall is well thought out.

First, there is information gathering.

"I'm going to go down to the capital tomorrow. Chat with Randall's brother in Algoa Road prison," Donnie informs us.

There's no love loss between Neil and Randall Ireland since Randall brained his brother with a baseball bat and basically "threw him under the bus," to take all the blame for their shared crimes against women. I don't know what kind of information Donnie thinks he'll get out of Neil.

Donnie has been talking to Davis and Jake, but I've only been half listening. My mind has left the present and has traveled back to how Neil used me and passed me off to his brother, Randall. I catch the end of Donnie's sentence, "I think he'll work a deal. Roll over on his brother. Neil has got to know something."

Second, is setting the trap.

"Dealing with a pervert stalker like Randall is like playing a giant live-action version of Whack-A-Mole. They disappear for an undeterminable amount of time. Like Randall. We haven't had a whiff of him in years and now BAM, he pops up. And that's the thing, you never know how long they're going to pop up. Just like Whack-A-Mole. It could be a long time OR it could be for a microsecond."

I interrupt, "Why now?"

"Who knows? It could be any number of things – money, you looked more accessible, he'd gone too long without a hit.

Now, it's Davis that interrupts, "A hit. A hit of what?"

Donovan turns his gaze toward me and up-nods. "Just what you think."

I inhale audibly. "I… I'm a hit?"

"To a stalker, the person they are stalking is a drug. And just like an addict, they can be 'clean' for a while, but the temptation to use, or in this case… obsess, is always there."

I don't know why I'm not freaking out, but I'm not. Right now, I want more information. I want to know what I'm up against.

"Eventually a pattern appears. One the 'mole' isn't even aware of. But the people watching, waiting… us, the police, finally see it and 'Whack!' the mole is trapped. Randall is just such a rodent."

Jake Gianni has been sitting quietly in our living room this whole time. Listening.

Davis turns his attention from Donnie Garrett. He diagonally nods his head upward in the direction of Jake's position on the couch. "So what's HE doing here?" He doesn't acknowledge Jake by his name or condescend to give him eye contact. It could take forever for Davis to forgive Jake for hurting me in college. Even though I already have.

"Jake?" Donnie asks.

Davis nods once.

"He's here to break up your marriage."

***

77

Jake and Donnie stand to leave. It's already six p.m. We've been strategizing all day. I've come to the stark realization in the past few hours that pretty soon, like in a day, my life will not be my own. At least for a while. I have tonight and tomorrow to be alone with Davis. After that, I'll be with him, but playing a role.

The only loose end in our operation is Randall Ireland. Like Carmen San Diego, we need to know where in the world he is. He was in Destin, Florida last night, and we presume this morning, but who knows.

The detective and Jake are practically to the door when my phone rings Boxwood's brand new hit. It's Charlie.

"Hey, Charlie Boxwood!" I answer brightly.

Charlie's greeting is less "greeting-y," "He's still here. Randall. Ireland."

I hold a finger up to Donnie, then cover the mouthpiece and whisper shout to him, "Randall's still in Florida." This brings both of the guys immediately back into the main seating area and Davis to my side.

I take my hand down, just as Davis asks, "How does he know for sure?"

Charlie hears Davis and I switch the phone to speaker and put it down on the coffee table, just as he answers. I can hear music in the background and lots of voices. "Jules had this idea. We threw sort of this impromptu pool party at the resort. You know how good Jules is at planning and publicizing events."

"Yeah." I say anxiously, wishing Charlie would move faster with his explanation.

"As soon as you left, she turned to me and said we needed to help you. Try to keep track of Randall. So she planned this party. We had the Georgia guys running all over the strip and mall and at every bar at lunch time handing out flyers advertising Boxwood doing an acoustic set here, at The Grand Jetty. Colin, Ian and Simon came down on the tour bus, after I called them. Anyway, long story short – we were playing and I saw him. He was on the other side of the pool enclosure scanning the crowd. It was so fucking strange, 'cause at first, I thought it was Davis. His hair is like Davis', except not as dark and he was wearing a GOOGLE shirt. I don't know anyone else with a GOOGLE shirt. Then I realized it was him. I think he was looking for you, Biz, because after about 15 minutes, he left. I saw him look at me and then find Jules and then he was gone. He knows you're not here anymore."

We – Davis, Jake, Donnie and I – are all leaning in, staring at the phone on the table. All of us, except the detective, with our hands steepled over our lips. I sense myself rocking at bit, but not frantically. Donnie has been listening intently and taking notes on his iPhone. He yells toward the phone, "When's the last time you saw him?"

Charlie says, "Uhm, about 30 minutes ago. We were in the middle of a set and I thought it would look weird if I just stopped."

Donnie looks at his watch, "That would have been a little after 5:30. Destin's in the same time zone, right?"

Having just been there, Davis and I simultaneously answer, "Yes, Central."

Donnie yells to Charlie on the phone again, "Thanks, Charlie. Tell your wife, tell Jules, she did good. This is good info. We can use this."

"Good. Glad it helped." Charlie replies.

I hear a movement on the other end and then my best friend's voice. She must have taken the phone from Charlie. "Biz, we're coming home tomorrow. We'll be there by evening. You okay?"

"I... you know... I think I'm as good as I can be. I'm really sort of surprising myself. Usually, with all that's been going on I would have had multiple meltdowns by now. But I... I just don't want to. It's so weird. Really... I'm just super, super tired." Upon hearing that, Davis moves closer to me on the couch and rubs my back gently and evenly.

"Get some rest!" Jules commands.

I tilt and turn my head to the right to make eye contact with Davis. I give him a tired smile. He reciprocates with his own and then runs his free hand through his hair. He's tired and worried, too. But still my gorgeous Mavis.

"K," I answer. "Goodnight."

"Goodnight. See you soon. Love you."

"Love you, too." And with that Jules and Charlie hang up.

Donnie has gotten up since asking Charlie his last question and is walking in circles around the seating area, tapping out something on his phone. We just watch him take a couple of turns, before he stops and announces, "If Randall left Florida immediately, depending on flights, he could be here as early as 10, 10:30. And by here, I mean here, at your door, not just in the city."

I stand up quickly, "You're kidding, right?"

"I wish I was. I don't think he could get here that fast. I'm checking flights now. There are no direct flights from that area, so that gives us more time. And best of all, he isn't in the vicinity now. Which means he hasn't seen Jake, or me. Which means he has no idea we've met. I think we have the jump on him." Donovan Garrett seems almost giddy. As giddy as a no-nonsense detective can get. "We're gonna get out of here, right Gianni?" Donovan addresses Jake.

"Yeah, I think it's time to get out of your hair, Biz... Davis." Jakes acknowledges each of us individually, "I'll see you Tuesday for lunch, Biz."

I wave and say, "Tuesday" to confirm.

Jake Gianni. My cover for this whole charade. And until recently, the last person I'd ever think of to ask for help.

And then something I never would have expected occurs, Davis moves from my side and walks the other two men to the door. Donnie walks out, but Davis stops Jake with some words I can't hear, leans in and says something more and then they shake hands. They actually shake hands and look, well, friendly. I'll have to ask Davis later what he said.

***

Davis and I are finally *completely* alone for the first time in two weeks.

"I thought we were going to have a movie night. Have popcorn," I warmly husk into Davis' ear, after he pulls me off from the couch and presses all of him against all of me. I wrap my arms around his neck by first slowly sliding them over his hard, muscular shoulders and then crossing them, so I can feel his delicious back with my hands. Davis responds by slipping his own arms slowly down the sides of my waist to settle at my lower back. He runs his thumbs under the waistband of the yoga pants I've traveled home in, and my panties.

"Isn't that what you used to always say your dorm room smelled like? Microwave popcorn?" Davis laughs with deep resonance into my shoulder. He kisses across my shoulder until he reaches my neck and then licks right up to my ear. A shiver runs down my spine and then a warming sensation overtakes me from the waist down and I feel my core flood in response.

I give a single low chuckle and tease back, "Until I found you, after that it smelled like sex and microwave popcorn."

Davis suddenly grabs my ass, lifts me up, and wraps my legs around his hips. I'm positioned perfectly on his hardness.

"Fuck the popcorn." Davis thrusts into me. I adore the feeling of his erection through the roughness of his jeans and the thin fabric of my yoga pants. I tilt my pelvis to ask for more. "And fuck the movie."

Davis takes a few long strides toward our bedroom with me as his enthralled passenger. With each step there is a stroke and release against my now pulsing clit. I thought I was too tired for any of this, but that's obviously not the case.

He moves us through the bedroom doors and I expect him to take me straight to our bed, but he doesn't. Davis turns and pushes my back against the wall just inside our bedroom door. One of his hands goes to my hip and he hikes me up and then grinds himself down my core vertically. I grind right back. His other palm slaps against the wall by my head. I am being held up only by the wall and one of his arms. His power to control me ignites the burning that's been kindling and I thrust my hands into his hair, pulling him into me. I want his mouth on mine. I want to consume him. It is not gentle. It is frantic. My lips open at the same moment as his and I pull his tongue into my mouth. I suck it with my lips and stroke it like I would his cock. I feel him harden further between my legs.

Still keeping me pinned securely to the wall with the force of his body and my legs like a vice around his hips, both of Davis' hands dive under my layered t-shirt and tank. They are peeled over my torso and I raise my arms quickly, grab the shirts with my hand and launch them over Davis' shoulder. He has flipped the cup down on one side of my bra and his mouth is on my nipple before I hear the shirts hit the floor. One of Davis' hands is back on my ass tugging me into... onto him and the other is cupping and massaging the breast he is suckling. I feel a jolt of what feels like pain, but also pleasure with each deep suckle and I groan. His suckles become lapping and then circular. I can feel them not only on my breast but lower, deeper. I sense my chest flush and both my nipples squeeze tightly and harden. Davis has worked the straps of my bra down and unfastened it. He slides it off one of my arms, then the other, all the while never allowing his lips to leave my body for more than a second.

As Davis ducks his head and pulls my other nipple deep into his mouth, I push into him and release my legs one at a time from around his hips. I slide myself down him, grasping at his powerful back and taking my time to drag my soaking self over him. I desperately need to have his pants off and have my hands on him. Once my feet hit the floor and I don't need to hold onto him so tightly, my hands fly to the buttons of his jeans. The pressure built against them from the strain of his imprisoned cock help me to pop them open with very little effort. As I push both this jeans and boxers down, he springs free.

Davis' mouth leaves my body and he takes a quick step back to free his feet from his jeans. He's about to lean forward to kiss me, but when he does, I take a quick lick of his lips and then drop to my knees. One of Davis' hands runs through my hair as I admire his rigid, throbbing cock right before my eyes. I stroke one of my cheeks and then the other against it, nuzzling and taking in the warm, earthy scent of Davis. Davis' hand moves to my chin and tilts my face up. I look up at him, smirk and raise my eyebrows. I lick my lips slowly and say, "Good idea... Fuck the popcorn," and then I dip my head for a more delicious snack. Davis' hands are in my hair, gently pressing my head toward him and away for awhile, but as I suck and stroke, moving from his thickened base up to the tip and then swirling back down, I feel his hands leave and slap against the wall in front of him. He is bracing himself. I feel the underside of his cock pulse between my lips. Davis is close.

As I increase the suction a bit more and drag my lips up to suck on the notch of his crest, Davis pushes off the wall, grabs my shoulders and brings me up so that I am face to face with him. Before I know what is happening, why he stopped me, Davis has thrown me across the bed and torn my yoga pants from my legs. I don't see any of it, rather just feel it since my head is hanging over the edge of the bed. My view is of my bedroom, upside down. I moan a bit and thrust up when two of Davis' long fingers enter me and his thumb pushes and then rotates on my clit. The "come here" stroke of his fingers on my G-spot is beckoning my release. I clench slightly, and when I release, Davis' fingers are gone, only to be replaced by his tongue taking the place of his thumb on my needy, ready, near-to-exploding clit. He licks me with a long deep stroke and then suckles and swirls, suckles and swirls. I feel my back begin to arch and my abdominals tighten. NO! If he can hold off so can I!

In a movement akin to doing a crunch, I sit up and pull Davis' head from between my legs. I push at his shoulders and position him on his back. Then I straddle him. I straddling his pulsing, rigid hardness and all the air escapes my lungs at once. "Aaaaaaah!" He feels so good inside me.

Davis pants out, "Jesus, Biz, you've never felt so hot. My God, you're on fucking fire inside. I'm going to combust."

All I can do is smile down at him. Davis is generally pretty quiet, so this declaration is something.

I ride him slowly, purposefully, never breaking eye contact. I know our nights together will be few after this week. This needs to be memorable. Davis moves and directs the motion of my hips for his maximum enjoyment with one hand, while his thumb rotates on my clit again.

I rock into him a few more times as I know I'm close to coming. Davis takes over, rolls me onto my back and begins to thrust rapidly. I lean up and kiss him passionately and then tell him, "Your cock has never felt more powerful inside me." And then I *really* feel the power as his lips open on top of mine, a loud guttural groan of pleasure is emitted and he jerks inside of me. My own orgasm follows as I involuntarily contract with force around him.

Chapter 12-Present: It Begins

Super security. That's what I have right now. Davis is always at home when I'm home. Donnie is always "somewhere" hovering around KTTA when I'm at work. I don't know exactly where, but I get cryptic texts from him telling me exactly what I'm doing and who I'm talking too. Just a tiny bit unnerving.

Lunches are spent with Jake Gianni. Even five years after meeting him, I can't deny he is very attractive, same highlighted hair and blue eyes. Now with a little sadness around them. I'd like to believe he would never treat any woman again the way he treated me. His assistance with the "Randall Situation" makes me feel he's changed. Lunch dates with Jake Gianni – Surreal. Surreal that Davis is cool with it.

I'm never alone.

But it's all part of a greater scheme. We have one week to set the scene and pull Randall Ireland in. One week until the Brandon-Connelly Foundation Gala.

Donnie's trip to Algoa Road Prison to visit Neil Ireland proved fruitful. Neil willingly gave information with Donnie's incentive of reduced time if he gave information that led to Randall's conviction. He admitted that Randall has always been very jealous of him. Even as kids there was terrible sibling rivalry for their mother's attention. Neil believes that Randall went far away after attacking him, but that he's closer to home now. Their mother told Neil she's receiving more frequent calls from Randall. The last few from either a 314 or 618 area code. This means he's in the bi-state area.

But so far, there has been no sign of Randall. It's once again as if he's disappeared. Donnie assures me it won't be for long – he'll pop up again. I'm not as confident.

***

Walking through the door of the condo after work, I'm immediately under olfactory attack. It smells like the garbage hasn't been taken out in days. I gag, involuntarily, several times and then put my hand up to my mouth and nose to block the odor.

"Babe… Davis…" I call out between retches.

"Yeah?" I hear from the direction of our home office.

Hearing Davis' footsteps, I question him before he's even in sight, "What is that horrible smell? Did you forget to take the garbage out?"

"I took it out this morning," Davis says as he approaches me. He stops suddenly in his tracks. "Pee-EEEwww. Man, that *is* a horrible smell. I didn't notice it earlier, but I've been in my office almost all day." He walks into the kitchen. I follow. Davis checks the garbage. It's empty.

"Wow" Davis muses, "I wonder what's causing that smell?"

I check the garbage disposal, the refrigerator and all the other trashcans. Davis is now following me around, sniffing the whole time. We are like a couple of bloodhounds on a mission.

"The smell is actually *stronger* over by the door," he says, like he's cracked the case. Davis opens the front door. I bug my eyes and nod in agreement, indicating I was already aware of that fact. "I can smell it in the hall, too." Davis walks out the door and then comes back in. "It seems to be coming from the garbage chute in the hallway. I'll call the condo manager and see what the issue is. I don't remember us having a garbage issue ever before."

I go to the hall closet to find some odor neutralizer and candles. Davis opens a few windows and turns on the whole-house fan. We go to our bedroom to escape, the now "floral garbage" smell, in the main part of the house. It takes about an hour, but when we finally stick our noses out, the smell has dissipated. At last – we can make dinner.

"You know what tonight is, right?" I ask Davis, as I pull the ingredients for our meal out of the fridge and cabinets.

Davis is slicing the meat for our dinner. Ginger beef with cellophane noodles. Elaborate sounding. Easy as can be to make. His cutting movements become less smooth and more choppy. "Yeah, I know. I was just not saying it out loud. You know that trick. You told me you used to do it. 'If I don't say it, it won't be true.'" Davis has not looked up from his task at the cutting board.

I move to him, depositing the other ingredients on the counter to free my hands. I place one hand over his hand on the knife to stop the now even more violent attack on the beef. "But really it is," I placate.

Davis puts down the knife and finally looks at me, "It's our last dinner at home alone. Our last night." His voice somewhere between anger and resignation.

I get as close to him as possible and put my hands on either side of his face, rubbing lightly to appreciate the scruff of his day-old beard. It's a sensation I associate with mornings and evenings at home with Davis. I'll miss it.

I whisper soothingly, "It's not really our LAST night. What we're doing… it's not forever…" I've been doing the same thing – pushing our inevitable separation out of my mind.

Davis leans his face into one of my hands and wraps an arm around my waist, pulling me closer. His gorgeous green eyes burn into mine with purpose.

"You're right, Lizard. Our forever hasn't even begun."

Chapter 13-Present: The Fundraiser Ball

"Rock 'n Fuckin' Roll!!"

Oh my god. He did it. He actually did it.

Charming Charlie. Charming Charlie Boxwood. He could yell out to a crowd, or even just whisper the most outrageous filth, so sweetly, he'd make a grandma titter like a schoolgirl with excitement. He did it. He actually said it. The F-bomb. At a Black Tie charity function. And you know what? When I look over my shoulder, I see the president of a regional hospital conglomerate mouthing the words, "Fuck, Yeah!" All these prim and proper society women are just smiling up at him for all they're worth. I shouldn't have worried – Charlie's going to kill it tonight!

Charlie bounds up to the mic and with both arms in the air, screams, "We are your hometown band, Boxwood, and we are here to make your night." He pauses for a bit and then adds, pointing a finger at one of the more mature women in the front, "Right, darlin'?" She actually screams his name. I swear to God, I wouldn't be surprised if a pair of Spanx landed on the stage at some point!

The Brandon-Connelly Foundation Gala tonight is equal parts exciting and bittersweet. Jules has created a sensational evening, and from what she's told me, Boxwood's performance is only one of the surprises. Little does she know Davis and I have a bit of a "surprise" of our own.

I look over to watch Davis watching the band. It's almost hard to believe I'm the one with the acting degree in this relationship, because he's doing a terrific job of playing the carefree husband and host. Davis is wearing his tux, a look I will never tire of. Tonight, it's with a regular tie, not bow. I enjoyed watching him get dressed. I slide my hand down his arm and he entwines his fingers with mine, doing the thing I like so much, the rubbing the thumb over my knuckles thing. Closing my eyes, I transport myself back to our condo a couple of hours ago. Something I think I'll be doing frequently over the next couple of weeks, or months. God, I hope it's not months.

Staring miserably at Davis' small suitcase placed next to the front door in the foyer, intellectually, I know tonight has to happen. Davis has to go away. But emotionally, it's gutting me.

Davis slides up behind me, I know because I can partially see his reflection in the foyer mirror as I glance up with a sigh. Davis puts his hands firmly on my hips, closes his eyes, gently rubs his nose in the back of my hair and sniffs quietly. He then puts his head down and kisses the top of my shoulder, right next to the intricate neckline of my black lace-over-blush Elie Saab gown.

"I always think you'll never be more beautiful to me. And then the next time I see you, you are. How do you do that?"

I turn to face him, my arms clutching his tux jacket at the sides. I smile tightly at his sweetness and completely ignore his question.

"Let's forget it. Let's not do it. I don't think I can be away from you. I've changed my mind. I don't care about Randall. Let the police figure it out." I am in full squirrel chatter mode.

"Biz, ssshhh." Davis bends slowly, tentatively and kisses me gently on the side of my mouth as I prattle on. "Now, you want to stop it? After all my initial hesitation. Lizard, we are going to do this thing and get it over with. And you… need to stop chattering. Because I'm this close…" Davis holds his thumb and forefinger together, right in front of my eyes to show me the exact measurement, "to taking you out of that pretty party dress and putting you right back where we've been all day – in bed."

"Davis…" I'm about to continue, but Davis' index finger presses firmly to my partially open lips.

"Come on. I need help with my tie. We can't be late to our own party."

I tie his black silk tie, the entire time thinking how he looks better without one. How he looks better without anything. The thought causes a slow burn to descend deep in my lower abdomen and I involuntarily tighten all the muscles in my pelvis.

"No, I guess you're right. We can't be."

I step away after finishing his tie and admire him. Then I turn back to the door, intentionally ignoring the suitcase. I pick up my crystal-covered clutch from the foyer table and start toward the front door.

I'm suddenly pulled backward and turned at the elbow. Davis has spun me around and is holding me slightly away from him. The perfect distance for his eyes to speak to me before he utters, "Biz? Tonight? When 'it' happens. Every time you hear me say something that hurts? Remember, I mean just the opposite. Every time you feel shock or pain in your heart? If that happens? Remember to replace that feeling with the feeling of my eyes on you right now. Replace it with thoughts of me kissing you, holding you. Remember, all my words tonight, no matter what they sound like, mean, 'I live for you. I. LOVE. YOU.' Can you do that?"

I kiss him. Our last private kiss. And breathe into him, "Yes."

"…great aren't they, Biz? Biz? Hey, where are you? Tahiti?" Davis jokingly snaps me back to the here and now by gently turning my head to pull my focus to his eyes, his words.

"No" I lean and whisper in his ear, "not Tahiti. Back at the condo."

"Aaahhh," he acknowledges my meaning.

***

Once my mind is completely back in the Starlight Roof Ballroom, I widen my view, take in the grandeur of the evening. All the men in their tuxedos and white dinner jackets. The women wearing some of the most gorgeous gowns I've ever laid eyes on. And the room? Perfection. The Starlight is probably one of the most exquisite venues in the whole city. It's on the top floor of The Chase Park Plaza. Floor-to-ceiling windows that look out over the lush and historic Forest Park and the twinkling city lights. There is a circular architectural feature with a window on the ceiling that makes it feel as if you are looking right up to heaven. Jules arranged to have wide swaths of white tulle draped in an array from the circular ceiling. It's all lit with pinks and corals and is giving the sunset now on display through the windows a run for its money. The large round tables are covered in the same colors with tall arrangements of white flowers in the center, making it possible to have a conversation even across the table. Jules has a gift for setting the right tone to make people loosen up – themselves and their wallets.

Boxwood finishes a song and Jules joins her husband on stage.

"Thanks, honey," she says to him and gives him a kiss on the cheek. Charlie escorts her closer to the mic by putting an arm around her waist and skootching her closer. He waves toward the mic, essentially inviting her to talk.

Jules talks to the crowd like she's sitting at my island in my kitchen talking to me, "I hope you all enjoyed dinner and the concert by Boxwood." People in the audience talk back to her, saying things like, "Yes, it was delicious," and "More Boxwood!"

She giggles and says, "Good. Sounds like you did. Well, we have more with Boxwood later. They are going to play another set later and there will be dancing." The crowd applauds loudly. "We have a special surprise now for the founders of this foundation. Davis. Biz. Will you please stand up and turn to the screen to the right of the stage."

I turn to Davis, "What's going on? What is this?"

Davis replies, "I have no idea."

We stand and smile, as the room breaks out in more clapping. And then the lights dim.

An image appears on the screen.

It is the First Lady of the United States!

I inhale audibly, grab Davis' arm and then look from the screen to Jules, who has one arm around Charlie and her other hand held up to her mouth in a fist. I know she is suppressing a scream. She releases her index finger from her fist and with it still at her lips, points to the screen.

"Hello, Davis, Biz, and everyone at the Brandon-Connelly Foundation NEVER AGAIN Gala. I'm so pleased to be here with you this evening, if only

*by video. I want to take a moment to honor the work that the foundation is doing to support young victims of sexual assault and those with mental health issues. The facts are: Young women still face the highest rates of dating violence and sexual assault, despite an increase in social awareness. One in five young women have been sexually assaulted while they're in college. It's everyone's duty to see that this appalling statistic is wiped out. We are proud to announce that the Brandon-Connelly Foundation and The White House will be teaming in the future to move the **1 is 2 Many** campaign forward."*

There is thunderous applause. I'm smiling so wide – so very proud of the work we are doing. I glance to Jules and give her a thumbs up.

The crowd quiets and the First Lady continues.

Some other facts: Suicide is the tenth leading cause of death in the U.S. (more common than homicide) and the third leading cause of death for people ages 15 to 24 years. One in 17 people suffer from serious mental illness, such as schizophrenia and bipolar disorder. One in 18 from anxiety disorders – social anxiety, panic disorder. I also have the honor of telling you, Biz and Davis, that the Brandon-Connelly Foundation has won a grant to support free screenings for mental illness on high school and college campuses."

Davis takes my hand and runs his thumb across my knuckles. In his touch are a million words and emotions. He looks down at me, just as I twist my head up and over my shoulder to look in his eyes. I know he's thinking about his brother, Cole, right now. Probably wishing he was here. I know I wish I could have met him.

The First Lady says her good-byes.

"Once again, thank you for inviting me to be a part of your evening. I'm excited to be working with you in the future. For those of you attending tonight, please be generous with this most important charity and have a wonderful evening. Congratulations and Good night."

Again, there is raucous applause.

As the lights come back up and the screen ascends, the partygoers become louder and more animated in their conversations. They surround Davis and me, asking if we knew about the First Lady's appearance. We didn't, of course. But Jules did. She has done everything in her power to make this a special evening. I almost allowed myself to believe for a moment that the evening was going to end well.

***

Davis and I dance to Charlie and the boys for a few tunes, then I lead him out to the open air portion of the roof. There is a light breeze and it's a bit cool for the beginning of May.

Once we are well away from other's ears, I turn to Davis and say, "It's been an almost perfect night – for the foundation, for Jules – I hate to ruin it."

"Almost perfect" Davis repeats my words. He's rubbing his hands up and down my arms to keep me warm. The skirt of my gown is rustling slightly in the wind. Davis' hair is blowing up a bit. He looks amazing. My mind flashes back to the first time I saw him in a suit – the Othello cast party – when I was with Jake. How's that for irony? Davis' eyes on my face warm me almost as much as his hands. I want desperately to kiss him, but I can't. It won't ring true with what we are about to do.

I tilt my head and pucker, kissing the air.

Davis up-nods like he's catching it. He presses his lips together and whispers, "Ready?"

"Never," I reply honestly but then say, "but, yes."

Here goes.

I take a deep breath, step back and scream angrily in his face, "NO!" loud enough for everyone on the terrace and in the ballroom to hear. And evidently they do, because my skin blushes with the burning of all their eyes on us. On me. I run from the terrace through the ballroom and into the lobby, just as we planned. I stop for a moment to let Davis catch up with me and grab my elbow, spinning me to face him. We are directly in front of the elevators. No one can get past us to leave. A captive audience to our "break-up."

Davis' face is full of anger. It looks so real, I'm shuddering a bit. And then it begins, "Really, Biz... Jake Gianni?! You've been seeing Jake-fucking-Gianni? I don't even believe this is fucking happening. You sure fooled me with your 'innocent victim' crap." I open my mouth to fake protest. No air escapes, but only an exhale. "I heard, I know…you've been seeing him and evidently some other guy. Jesus, Biz! Don't *I* feel like an idiot." His voice has gotten louder and rougher and more full of hate. I have to actively remind myself this is an act and that his words mean nothing. That I'm supposed to imagine him telling me he loves me.

It's barely working. Big, fat salty tears are building in my eyes and just as one falls down my cheek, I not so fake beg, "Davis, please, it's not what you think… Jake is nothing to me."

"Oh, well that makes it even worse. You're fucking around and it means nothing," Davis growls realistically "You really are a slut!"

Wow! Those words hurt more than I believed possible.

I plead, "Davis, I love you. I'm sorry. Really…it's NOT. WHAT. YOU. THINK." I sob between each of my last words.

This is feeling too real. It hurts too much. And just when I think I can't take another moment, Davis fires the killing shot.

"I'm DONE, Biz. DONE. I won't be home tonight."

He pushed the elevator button right before he said it and like magic it arrived. After delivering his last word, he steps into the elevator and is gone.

My head is swirling. That went well. Too well. It was all too real. And painful. All the air has left the room. It's eerily quiet. It seems Davis left an entire room speechless with this faux venom. Not wanting to face anyone, I run to the stairwell, slip off my silk blush-colored Gucci crystal ankle straps and run down the stairs as fast as one can in a couture gown. I cannot help the sobs heaving from my mouth. It was all an act, but my heart is having trouble accepting that fact, even if my head knows the truth. If there was anyone in the crowd not fooled by our performance, I'd be amazed.

I run out of the building in tears, ensuring everyone in my wake sees me, and slide into the seat of my waiting Town Car. Donovan had it arranged to be ready and waiting. None of this public "break-up" has been left to chance. Even Kathleen, our friend at Arch Scene magazine and Smitty, her boyfriend/photographer, were tipped off.

The valet begins to close the door. As he does, I hear him say, "Don't worry, Biz. Your husband is an idiot. There's someone better out there for you. I'm sure you'll see them soon."

I know the voice. I look up as the car door closes and through the window, staring at me intensely, is Randall Ireland. Dressed as a valet. Those narrowed, creepy eyes are unmistakable. A smile spreads slowly across his face. He winks and the car takes off. My head turns, as we pull away, not able to take my eyes off him, like I've seen a dead person come to life.

Now really panicked, I dig in my clutch for my cell phone and text Donovan.

The mole has popped up

***

"Let him go, Biz… It's time for Davis to go," Donovan insists from behind me placing both of his hands on my shoulders. I'm clutching Davis with all my might. Davis has one hand around my waist, the other is holding his suitcase. The one I was staring at earlier in the evening. We are standing in the foyer of our condo and I'm clinging to him like my life depends on it. When the car let me out, I ran up the stairs and into our condo, straight into Davis' arms. And that's where we are now. I almost missed him. Almost missed holding him one more time before he left. Our foreheads are together, our eyes burning into each other. Davis opens his mouth to say something, when our front door flies open, slamming into the wall. I feel Donnie's hands leave my shoulders and he moves to stand in front of us, his hand reaching into the left side of his jacket at the same time. Is he reaching for his gun?

"I'm going to fucking kill him!! What the fuck does he think he's doing?!"

Charlie barrels into our condo with Jules in tow, tottering behind him on her four-inch heels, her perfect coif falling down. He looks like he ran the few blocks from the hotel. Breathing hard. Sweating. And the look on his face – like he could tear someone's heart out with his bare hands. Jules' expression is worse.

Charlie stops just inside the door, perhaps at the seriousness of Detective Garrett's position as a human shield. "Davis?" Charlie growls.

Simultaneously, Jules says, her voice high and squeaky with concern, "Biz, What is going on? Are you guys really breaking up?"

Donovan turns to Davis and me and says, "It's up to you, guys. The more people that know the more complicated this will be." He's right, but we can't leave our best friends in the dark.

I nod at Donnie and he steps aside. Davis and I hold hands and face Jules and Charlie. We look at each other one more time. In that look is confirmation of our agreement. Charlie makes a quick move toward Davis his hand up and fisted.

"Charlie, no!" I yell.

Jules pulls on Charlie's arm, silently directing him to lower it.

Davis puts both hands up, taking on the posture of surrender "Charlie, man, don't. Don't be pissed. We aren't breaking up. It was an act…"

"An act?" The hurt is front and center in Jules' voice.

Charlie steps back and places both hands on the sides of his forehead, while shaking his head, "What the fuck, guys?

It's my turn to talk.

Donnie is pacing impatiently off to the side. I know he wants us to hurry. I can hear him mumbling, "Wasting time."

I speak rapidly. Everyone knows I'm really good at talking rapidly, especially when nervous or panicked. Which, right now, I am. "Charlie, Jules, we don't have much time. Here it is. Davis and I faked breaking up. We're trying to get Randall Ireland to come out of hiding, show himself. Donnie…" I turn and point to the detective, "had the idea that if we broke up publicly, Randall would find out and show up. It's working. He was at the Gala, posing as a valet. I saw him and he talked to me. We have to get Davis out of here. We have to make this look real. Do you understand?" They nod that they do. "Can you help us?" They nod again.

"NOW!" Donovan interjects emphatically. He's serious now. Waving us toward the door.

Wordlessly, because really, what more can we say, Davis and I kiss. The kiss is good-bye, a promise to see each other soon and the desperate making of a memory all at once. Davis backs away from me, not releasing my hand until the last possible moment. I see Donnie walk over to Charlie and whisper something in his ear. Davis walks out the door. He can't be but one or two steps out when I see Charlie bolt after him.

Then, from the hall a barrage of profanity and loud argument occurs – Charlie is ripping Davis a new one. "I am going to fucking KILL YOU, Davis Brandon. Seriously, you think you can talk to my sister that way!"

I hear Davis reply, "She's not your fucking sister!"

WAIT! My heart screams to my brain before the word escapes my mouth.

"Wait!" I move toward the door to stop Davis.

Donnie grabs me by the shoulders and stopping me with a ferocious glare tells me, "No! It starts NOW!"

I didn't hear it. Davis didn't say it before he left. He always says it to me. Every time we part. "HAVE FUN." It doesn't mean exactly what it sounds like. It can mean whatever we need it to at the time. And he didn't say it. This is not good. Not good at all. For the first time in a long time, I give into the panic and begin to cry. Donovan pulls me into his arms and up against his large chest to silence the tears as they come. My expensive mascara is no match for this night. I am certain Donnie's shirt will be covered with black streaks.

I feel Jules come up behind me and run her hand down the back of my hair. Then she turns me out of the detective's embrace and into hers. "Sshh, Sshh… I got you. *I* got you, now." From the tone of her voice, I get the sense she was talking to Donnie Garrett with her last words, not me.

Chapter 14-Present: Four Weeks In

It DOES feel like forever. Forever since I've seen Davis. Held Davis. And it's only been four weeks. Four weeks with no direct contact. That's the rule. NO Contact. I have not spoken, texted, Face-timed, emailed, snail-mailed or seen my husband directly. I know he's been out on tour with Boxwood some of the time. Mostly because I have their tour schedule memorized. And Jules tells me. All communication is filtered through Donnie or Jules and it's been minimal.

Frequently I open up the website for the Boxwood/Lawnmower Tour, hoping a picture of Davis will appear. It's also one of the only times during these days apart that I laugh, recalling Davis joking about how *Boxwood/Lawnmower Live!* sounds more like a gardening exposition than a rock concert. The corners of my lips turn up into the kind of smile that only Davis can put on my face when think I about him saying the tour should be called the "Trimming the Hedges" Tour. I miss his dirty mind and his double entendres.

This separation is worse than when we spent a summer apart. Almost worse than when I was so very alone – before I ever met him. I wonder how much longer I can hold out.

By all appearances, to those not in the very small circle "in the know," I am living the life of a happy, newly separated woman.

Couldn't be further from the truth.

But as I've heard from Davis before, "people's perceptions are their reality," even if it's not the truth. An outsider's reality of my current status might go something like this: Biz Connelly is a slut.

Yeah, I could see that it would look that way. It's what we want Randall's reality to be.

I have "dates" two times a week with Jake, two times a week with Donovan. Sometimes on the dates, we go out. Other nights, Jake or Donnie will come over and spend the night. These nights are the best. Not because I'm enjoying a romantic evening with one of my new lovers. Ha! No, they sleep on the couch. More like, I don't have to get dressed up, I don't have to pretend and I get to go to bed early. It also ensures that I'm protected. This ruse is exhausting. That's the reality. Much less scandalous than the illusion we're creating. I hope to God, Randall is paying attention and buying it, because I don't know how much longer I can do this.

Oh, and my condo continues to smell like garbage. At least two or three nights a week.

***

One evening, one of Donnie's nights to stay with me, I asked him what his wife thought of all this – her husband fake dating another woman. Staying out all night.

He sort of grunted and laughed at the same time and said, "She doesn't know."

"What do you mean, she doesn't know?" I probe.

"I'm at work. That's what she knows. She knows what I do. She doesn't ask questions. Once I close a case, I tell her, if she asks. Right now, she knows I'm working on the Randall Ireland case. That's all. Not everything," Donnie explains as he sits down on the sofa and flips on the news, not looking at me as he talks. This is my date tonight.

Then he adds, with as much affection as I've ever seen this gruff police detective display, and a soft sigh, "Posey. She's my good girl." I can tell in those few words he adores his wife.

***

Randall has not made himself visible in a month. The last time I saw him was the evening we began this whole thing. Donnie says it's time to step up the game. I need to go out more. And – I need to start picking up and dating random guys. It's supposed to give Randall the impression that I'm open to more options than just the two guys I'm "cheating" on my husband with.

I give Donnie an ultimatum, "Three weeks. That's it. I can't do this much longer. Three weeks."

Donnie only nods his agreement.

Chapter 15-Present: Five Weeks In

There is an old Shriner's temple near our condo. As part of the urban renewal our city is undergoing, it has been converted to a movie theatre. But not just any sort of movie theatre. This one is upscale, with a Middle Eastern flair. The theatre doesn't have small, sticky theatre seats, but luxurious, reclining couches, perfect for snuggling. In the large, gorgeous Temple Bar in the lobby there aren't regular tables and chairs. No, there are low tables with large silk cushions in saturated jewel tones around them, scattered on top of oriental rugs. The place is intimate and mysterious and has become a popular date destination. A popular trysting destination. Tonight, I pick up my first "random guy." The random guy hand selected by Donovan Garrett from all the undercover cops in his precinct. All I know is the guy's name is Aaron. According to Donovan, he has thick dark brown curly hair and wears glasses. He'll be wearing jeans, a navy blue and white striped t-shirt and flip-flops. At first, I snickered at Donnie's very specific description. Then I realized, he's a detective. It's his job to be specific.

I order a cocktail. It's a move out of character for me, but I'm trying to give the impression that I'm "running wild." The Temple Bar has become well known for its cocktails, so I order one of their signature drinks – a Marrakesh Pineapple Smash. One sip and I know it's strong, whiskey-based, and dangerous. Fortunately, my "date," approaches not long after and engages me in conversation.

Moving in close, he says so only I can hear, "Hi there, Ms. Brandon. I'm Aaron." I shake his hand and gesture for him to sit.

"Please, call me Biz," I say giddily.

I quickly abandon the drink and focus on Aaron. I'm surprised how easily acting comes back to me. He is soon whispering in my ear. To anyone walking by, they'd think he was whispering sweet, dirty nothings to me. I giggle, as if he's said something incredibly clever. What he's really telling me is the plan for tonight. Aaron, suddenly, suggests loudly that we go in to see the movie. I agree. He helps me up to my feet from the cushions.

I straighten my skirt and as I look up, I see not Aaron, but Davis.

"Biz?" Davis says. I see a spark of excitement in his eyes. Oh, I've missed his beautiful green eyes looking into mine.

I can say nothing. No words are forming. Firstly, because I haven't seen my husband in over 30 days. And secondly because he's standing in front of me, in the lobby, on an obvious date with… Suzette.

The skank. Jake's Ex. My former RA colleague. And worse of all, a childhood friend of the Ireland brothers. I'm stuck where I stand. No words will form. I must look like I've had a lobotomy because my thoughts, never mind words, won't come together.

Suzette? What is he doing with her?

Aaron steps forward and says to Davis, "Hey, I'm Aaron. Are you a friend of Bizzy's?" Wow! Aaron has done his homework. Using a familiar version of my name so quickly.

Davis looks confused, but shakes Aaron's hand, "Uh, yeah, we're… friends."

Suzette chimes in bitchily, "Friends? Oh my God, Biz is Davis' wife. Or should I say soon to be ex-wife."

Aaron looks at me in shock. If he's done his homework, he already knows I'm married… then oh, he is good at his job… *really* good. The shocked look is all part of the act.

I finally regain my faculties and stutter out an introduction, which I quickly realize is redundant, "D-Davis, this is Aaron… Oh, you already know that."

"Yeah" is all Davis says. His eyes dull and he continues, telling us, "Well, we've got to get into the movie."

Suzette takes Davis' hand and pushes her upper body into his arm suggestively. Like practically rubbing her breasts on him, suggestively. They turn and leave. Davis looks over his shoulder at me. At first, I think I see yearning and then blankness.

I whisper, "Bye," at him. I don't think he heard me.

My head is in a flat spin. I've wrapped my arms around my waist to hold myself together. Once Davis and Suzette are out of sight, I let a rushed anguished sound escape my lips.

Aaron rapidly moves to my side and has an arm around my waist. I wish it was Davis' arm. "You okay?" he asks.

"No." I snap at him. I want this "date" to be over now.

Aaron leans down and says very, very quietly directly into my ear, "Don't worry. Your husband's date tonight is fake, too." I sigh in relief. He did know! Aaron knew it was my husband. I wonder if Davis knew. And what's with Suzette? Why is she Davis' beard? Is it because she knows the Ireland brothers? Is she "in the know" or could Davis and Donnie just be using her to feed info to Randall? My cortex is swirling with a million questions. I wonder if she knows her date is phony? Aaron continues, "Now, put your head on my shoulder and act like you're having a great time."

I do as I'm told.

***

The movie is The Great Gatsby and much as I enjoy "eye-touring" Leo DiCaprio, I cannot stay awake. The recliners are comfortable, I'm exhausted from work, I'm exhausted from "play dating," it's dark, I've had a cocktail and Aaron's arm is warm around me. The outcome of all of these factors is me in a deep snooze on his shoulder.

I only know I've been sleeping when Aaron says, "Ms. Brandon? Biz?" gently by my ear. I jerk awake with a start. The movie is ending. As the credits begin to roll the other patrons in the audience get up to leave. I wipe the drool from my lip and apologize to Aaron, trying to paw away the little bit that also puddled on his shirt.

"Oh my God, I'm so sorry. I didn't mean…"

I stop talking. That weird garbage-y smell hits me and my stomach flips. I cover my nose and mouth with my hand to conceal a retch. From beneath my hand, I ask Aaron in muffled speech, "Did you smell that?"

"What?" he asks.

I describe it to him. "A smell. Like garbage… and maybe cigarettes, alcohol… Just garbage-y."

Aaron finally seems to catch a whiff of it. "Oh, yeah. Wow! Someone in here has really bad b.o."

So it's not just me. I was beginning to think I was imagining it. The smell really is in here. And Aaron thinks it's a person. I take my hand down from my mouth. The smell has dissipated.

"Come on, Biz. Let's get you home," my date tells me, looking in my eyes with realistic seductiveness. Oh, that's right. I'm on my mock pick-up-a-random-guy date. Which includes a mock hook-up at my place.

***

"Aaron, you can sleep in the guest room. Obviously, by my sparkling company and the drool stain on your shoulder, I'm wiped out. I'm going to sleep. Thanks for helping out with this plan." I yawn and then add quietly, "Even if it doesn't pan out."

Aaron waves good night and moves in the direction of the room I just pointed out to him. I'm not being a very good hostess, but right now I don't care. I just want to sleep. I think I need a day off to catch up on my rest. Get on top of this crushing fatigue.

***

Walking out of my bedroom after sleeping like a rock, I yawn and spy a really buff back on a half naked dark haired guy sitting at the island of my kitchen. For half a beat, I think its Davis. I know its Aaron with the second half of that beat.

Back still to me, Aaron greets me. "Good Morning, Biz. Did you sleep well?"

I wipe my eyes and zip up my hoodie a little higher, "Umm, yeah, as a matter-of-fact, I did."

He turns. Whoa! I miss my husband and I'm sick of this whole sting to catch Randall, but whoa! Aaron's chest. It's so… so… chiseled. I stare. Probably a little too obviously, because Aaron reaches over to the chair next to him and proceeds to put on the button up shirt he arrived in last night.

Peeling my eyes off him, I go into the kitchen for coffee. I'm beginning to think I shouldn't interact with him before I've had coffee.

Aaron chuckles softly. I guess he did notice my gawking. "Good. I mean, good that you slept well, because I just got a text from Garrett." Aaron holds up his cell phone. "Randall, or someone looking like him, was seen last night."

"What?" I say and turn quickly, spilling a bit of coffee on my hand. It burns a bit. I place the cup on the counter and run cold water over it in the sink.

"Yeah, evidently when we were leaving the theatre, one of the patrols that were watching outside spotted a guy that fit his description," Aaron continues, getting off the barstool and coming over to take my hand, "Let me look at that burn."

I pull my hand away and snap, "It's fine." It is fine. And I don't want some half naked hot guy touching me. I want Davis. "Tell me more about Randall."

"It looks like he was hovering around the theatre last night. So maybe this plan of Garrett's is working after all."

Chapter 16-Present: Six Weeks In

Over the next week, a person, now almost one hundred percent sure to be Randall, has been observed lingering outside KTTA and buying liquor at the local drugstore near my condo. He's popping up and staying up, just as Donnie predicted. Maybe this will be over soon.

I continue with my frequent dating of Jake, Donnie, Aaron and a few other random "pick ups" that Donnie arranges. Donnie keeps trying to get me to agree to let this continue past seven weeks. I'm firm in my resolution that it ends soon. I'm worn down. Working all day. Out every night. No contact with the man I love, except for some vague third-party messages from Jules that he's okay and he loves me. I only sleep somewhat well if one of the cops are staying over. I feel less safe with Jake, somehow. He didn't have to help on this and I could be putting him in danger.

Jake and I arrive back at the condo on a Wednesday. Once he closes the front door, I throw my purse on the sofa and collapse next to it with a sigh. Another date over. In that moment, I get the nerve to ask him what I've been wondering. "Jake, why are you helping with this? What do you get out of it?"

Jake looks down at the floor in the entryway, not coming any further into the condo. "I treated you really badly, Biz… back in college. If I wasn't such an asshat, I might be where Davis is now. I might not have two failed marriages. I might have someone that really cares for me. I might have been… yours."

It's so sweet and sad. "Oh, Jake."

Neither of us moves.

"I'm not trying to creep you out or hit on you, Biz."

"I know."

"I don't know exactly why I'm doing this... I just need something good to happen in my life. I thought maybe if I helped you, things would turn around. They sort of already have," Jake confesses.

I perk up. "What do you mean?"

"Well, you know how sometimes I pick you up from KTTA to go out?"

"Yeah."

Jake blushes and continues. "Umm. I've sort of been... talking... like just having a few conversations with your boss, Gail... and uh, well, I think I like her."

Gail is probably twelve or fifteen years older than Jake. I'm not judging. I just didn't expect this.

Jake's still standing in the entry. "Biz, after all this is over... do... do you think you could put in a good word for me. You know, with Gail."

I smile and stand up. "Sure, Jake." I turn to go to my bedroom. I stop and say over my shoulder, "You with Gail. Cool. I just hope I can put in that good word soon. 'Night, Jake. Thanks for the date."

"No problem" Jake replies. I hear him walking to the guest room. "'Night, Biz."

Pajamas. I just want to get into my ratty old Hello Kitty PJ bottoms, crawl into bed and dream of Davis. I think he is in Oklahoma with Charlie and the guys tonight. I need to check the tour itinerary on my phone before I go to bed. I hope Davis is receiving all the telepathic messages I'm sending him, since those are the only ones I'm sending or receiving. As I step into our walk-in closet, my eyes for some reason, hone in on the Agent Provocateur bag that is on the floor next to some of my shoes. This reminds me of two things: I must be hanging my head in self pity if my focus is on the floor AND I didn't get to wear my sexy lingerie named Whitney for Davis yet. I was going to wear it for the gala, but that was just too sad to even consider seriously. I don't even look in the bag. I just kick it further back behind more shoes so I don't have to see it the next time I come in. I exhale and visualize the countdown calendar of when I can be with Davis again, then I grab my tank top and PJs.

All this ends in eleven days, whether Randall is caught or not. Eleven days and I can have the man I want in my condo, in my bed. Davis. Not imposters for my affection on a rotating schedule.

***

On the calendar app on my iPhone I have a countdown calendar. Nine days until the end of this debacle. While Randall has shown up around town a little more, he has disappeared back into his hole just as quickly. I'm losing confidence and patience.

Tonight, I'm supposed to go out with Jake again. I don't have to come back to the office until Monday, but I have some work to do over the weekend, so I grab everything off my desk including my unopened mail. I figure I can look at it at home before Jake arrives.

No one is around as I walk out the back entrance of KTTA to my little red-with- white-stripes Mini Cooper. It's not the car I ever would have thought of for myself, but when I saw it on the lot and drove it, I fell in love. Donnie Garrett told me he was glad, evidently it makes me easier to keep track of – for the police and Randall. Conspicuous.

I plop into the driver's seat of the car and throw my purse and my bag with work papers on the passenger seat. As it lands, a large white envelope pops out and I see it's addressed to BUSY CONNELLY. That's weird. Most people that know me well, spell my name correctly. And know I'm married. I pick up the envelope and see that the return address has nothing but a name. The name is IRELAND. My first thought is, "Why would Neil Ireland be writing to me?" It's quickly replaced with, "No, not Neil. Randall." Instinctively, I lock the car doors and survey the area around me in the parking lot. Still nobody around. Tearing the envelope open, I pull out a single sheet of paper. On it is a picture of Randall. Hair longer, darker, not reddish anymore. He's wearing one of Davis' t-shirts or one that looks just like it, the one I threw out months ago. I wonder where he got it. I notice that my breathing has gotten faster and shallower. I'm feeling lightheaded and my upper lip is sweating. Then I read the short typed message under the picture.

Bizzy, I see you're getting BUSY all over town. How about adding me to the rotation?

Contact me by Twitter

And there it is, his twitter account address.

I fumble in my purse for my phone to call Donovan. He needs to know this, immediately. I need him to meet me at the condo. I get it out and see there is a message from Jules.

Davis wants to meet you. He said he's sick of not seeing you.

He'll be waiting at the apartment. He said he doesn't care what Det. Garrett says, he's going to see you.

I reply back:

Really? I'm on my way.

What? This is so strange. I call Donnie and tell him about the note from Randall. He agrees to meet me at the condo to strategize what to do next. He thinks we should make contact. I also break it to him that Davis has had enough and will be waiting at the condo for me. Donnie is not pleased with that development. I assure him Davis will be careful. I'm not really sure how careful Davis is being, but I'm covering for him so the detective won't be so pissed. I make one more request.

"Donnie, do you think I could have like five or ten minutes alone with Davis before you get there?"

"BIZ!" Donnie sounds aggravated.

I plead, "Please Donnie, just five or ten minutes. I haven't seen Davis in so long."

"You saw him a week ago."

I huff out, "You know what I mean. I was on a fake date. He was with Suzette. We exchanged, like five words. That doesn't count."

Donovan Garrett is quiet on the other end of the phone. He's either angry or thinking. I hope it's the latter. I match his silence.

Suddenly he gruffs out, "Five minutes."

I beg for more, "Ten?"

"Five." And with that Donnie hangs up.

My mind is racing. One thought tumbling and tripping over the next. Randall is out there. Close by. He wants me to contact him. This could be the break we need.

And, Davis is waiting for me at home!

Chapter 17-Present: Davis Is Home

I park my Mini in my parking spot. Looking over at Davis' spot, I notice that his Lexus isn't there. That's probably a good thing. It means he walked or took a cab or had someone drop him off. Scooping up all the papers that fell out and shoving them back in my bag, I fling it over my shoulder, along with my purse. After checking to see if anyone is in the garage, I unlock the door, get out and practically sprint to the elevator.

The door to the elevator opens and I want to run down the hall to my place, to Davis. I don't, because when I step out, it's right into a waft of stink. The horrible garbage smell is in the hallway. Garbage and old alcohol – like the way the back alley of a bar smells. I walk over to the garbage chute. I push it open – it's the exact smell. I make a mental note to talk to the head of the condo association. I continue down to my door, the smell not going away as I get closer. In fact it seems stronger.

I open the door to the condo, expecting to see Davis right there waiting for me, in his usual place, leaning against the back of the sofa that faces away from the door. He's not there. I call out, "Mavis? Babe?"

I hear a muffled, "In here," coming from the guest room. Why is he in there? Why isn't he out in the living room or waiting in our bedroom? My rational mind tells me its because Davis is trying to be careful. He's trying to see me on the sly without Randall knowing. Makes sense.

After throwing all my stuff, including my cell phone, over the back of the sofa, I go to the guest room and push open the door.

No Davis.

"JULES!" I scream at the sight of my best friend. Jules is sitting on a chair. NO, she's tied to the chair. Her mouth is covered with duct tape.

She's violently shaking her head "No," fear radiating out of her eyes. I take a few steps into the room intent on freeing her from the duct tape over her mouth and the ropes tying her arms and legs. "Oh my God! What's going on? Where's Davis?"

Jules' head is still shaking back and forth violently.

The door slams shut behind me and I spin to see why, before I've reached Jules.

Randall Ireland is standing between the door and me.

Sneering. Dirty.

And smelling like garbage. And alcohol.

The garbage smell. It was Randall! In my house. At the movie theatre. Randall has been everywhere I've been. Maybe even while I was there!

"Hey Biz. Biz-zy," Randall drawls in his oily voice. "You know, I just couldn't wait for you to tweet me, so I came on over."

"Randall" I almost silently whisper in disbelief.

He just keeps talking, slurring really, "Yeah, it's me. I figured you'd be sick of those other guys by now and need a real man to get you off. I kinda know how Davis feels. I was gettin' 'sick of waiting' to see you too." Randall holds up a cell phone that I recognize as Jules'. It's open to the text she just sent me. The one he just quoted. It takes me a few moments to come to grips with this fact: Davis isn't coming. He never texted me through Jules. Randall kidnapped Jules and texted me himself!

Jules' muffled screams bring my attention back to her. I turn my head to see her wriggling in the chair. I'm afraid to turn my back on Randall, but I need to help my friend. I make the decision to get Jules' free. She's pregnant and scared. I turn and take only one step toward her. Jules is shaking her head even more violently. I don't make it anywhere close to her when I'm pulled backward by an arm around my waist. My mouth is covered by a hand. Randall's hand. He pulls my head back causing a shooting pain in my neck. I scream into Randall's hand ineffectively. He drags me backward out of the guest room, away from my friend. Away from her even more terrified eyes. At least I know she isn't in immediate danger anymore.

I am.

Randall stops, takes his hand off my mouth and I scream out Jules' name.

He hisses in my ear after spinning me quickly and pulling me roughly up against him. "Shut the fuck up, Biz! Your friend can't help you. Your 'date,' Jake isn't coming. It's just you and me now. No Neil. No Davis. YOU. AND. ME. The way it was always supposed to be."

I can't stop shaking. This lunatic is full-on crazy. I'm seriously in trouble. My only glimmer of hope is that Donovan is true to his five-minute edict. *Why isn't he here yet?*

"Strip!" Randall commands.

I try to pull away from him and scream, "NO!" My voice is thin and scared sounding. Just hearing it frightens me more. I have no control in this situation. *Where are you, Donovan?*

Randall tears open my button-up dress shirt and bellows again, "Strip! Now!"

I don't know what else to do. If I strip slowly, Donovan might get here before I'm done. I reach for my shirt and look down to see a gun pointed right at my chest. A big, black, square gun. Davis' gun. The one Randall took from him at the skatepark. Right in front of me. Pointed at me. I begin to shake all over involuntarily.

Randall growls, "I fucking said, 'Strip!' Biz. What the fuck are you waiting for?"

Randall pokes at my now only bra-covered chest with the barrel of the gun nudging me backward into the living area. I'm standing in the middle of the room and he sits on an ottoman. The same ottoman Davis sat on when I stripped for him for fun. Bile slides up my throat. I swallow it down. Not looking at Randall, but with my eyes fixed on the seam where the wall and ceiling meet behind and above him, I robotically remove my shirt and drop it on the floor.

"You can do a fuck ton better than that, Biz. I've seen you out with your boyfriends. Turn it on. Seduce me." He now has one hand on the gun, pointed at me, and the other cupping his dick over his pants.

I continue to stare above him, tears now rolling steadily down my cheeks and sobs escaping my throat. *I can't believe Donnie isn't here yet. WHERE IS HE?*

"Goddamn, you're hot. Now take off that skirt." I do. "And the shoes," Randall barks out. I look at him only briefly and see he is stroking himself. God, I could vomit. "Fucking, black underwear... I can't wait to rip that shit off of you." My tears come unabated now. I'm hyperventilating. The room spins. Randall stands up quickly, grabs me by the elbow, in a move similar to the one that dislocated my shoulder under the bridge at the skatepark, where we had our last confrontation, and pushes me face first over the arm of the sofa. I'm completely vulnerable. My ass is in the air and my face is smashed against the seat cushion. Randall runs the gun barrel down my spine, stopping just above my panties. I gulp down the impeding vomit and try to focus through my blinding tears.

"You are so fucking gorgeous, Biz. The years apart have only made me want you more. I didn't screw you last time because I wanted you present. Not unconscious. But this time, you're not drugged. I'm not just going to play with you like I did last time." Randall continues in a menacing sing-song, "Oh no, I am gonna FUCK you. And you are going to love it!" An ear-piercing howl rips out of me when I hear him pull down the zipper on his jeans.

Chapter 18-Present: Davis Is Home, Part 2

The front door slams open so loudly it sounds like it's been bashed in. I throw my head up from the cushion of the couch and see Donovan Garrett, only feet away, directly in front of me, gun drawn and pointed at Randall.

"Freeze!" he yells. Donovan begins to slowly move forward, "Randall Ireland, you are under arrest. Drop your weapon and move away from Ms. Brandon…"

I no longer feel the gun barrel on my back and then I hear shots. I can't keep track of how many. I ducked my head with the first one, but now they've stopped and I look up. Donnie Garrett is on the floor leaning against the table in the foyer. There is blood covering his left shoulder, but his gun is still up and pointed over my head. I hear unintelligible screaming and see a gun next to the sofa. I reach down and grab it. It's the gun Randall had.

In a weakened yell, Donnie says, "Biz! Get up! Behind you!" I scramble to my feet and spin around in the direction Donnie's gun is pointed. Without thinking, I bring the gun I am holding up and point it in the same direction. Before me is Randall, screaming, holding his right hand with his left. Blood is pouring down his arm. He lunges toward me. I move to the side, he falls and now it is Randall over the arm of the sofa.

I don't know what overtakes me, but I'm suddenly not scared. No, I am FILLED with rage. The roles are now reversed and I stick the gun barrel down onto Randall's neck. I growl at him, "I should kill – "

Davis' voice stops me. "Biz, don't."

The gun still pointed at Randall, I glance up to see Davis in the open doorway to our home. I have to be dreaming. Dreaming in the middle of a horrible nightmare. Standing paralyzed, in my underwear, splattered with blood, in a dream, in a nightmare. I can't speak.

Donovan yells to Davis, "She's in shock, man! Get my cuffs, get them on Ireland and get that gun away from her."

"You're hurt." I hear Davis say to Donovan.

"Never mind about me. Go to Biz!"

Davis slowly moves to the opposite side of the couch. I maintain eye contact with him, even though I am still very much aware that I have the gun pointed at Randall. Davis' eyes are the only thing holding me together. The feeling I have when I'm in a panic attack is upon me, but not physically. Just inside. Inside I think I will shake and crack into a million pieces. On the outside, I am granite.

I hear the sound of metal handcuffs ratcheting closed. I look down and see Randall flailing side-to-side on the sofa, but unable to move really. He's still screaming, but none of it makes sense to me.

There's a hand on my arm.

"Give me the gun, Biz. You don't want to do that." It's Davis. Davis is talking to me. I think I might not be dreaming. I don't know. I'm so confused.

"Davis?"

"Yeah?"

"I think I could have killed him. I really think I wanted to kill him…" I cry out.

Davis' hand is over mine on the gun, "Let go," he says calmly.

I let go. Davis takes the gun. Suddenly, the room is filled with people in uniforms and noise and more screams from Randall, I think. There is movement everywhere. Randall has been pulled off the couch by two police officers. They are reading him his rights, *You have the right to remain silent. Anything you say can and will be used against you in a… "*

The room spins and begins to darken. I put my hand up to my mouth. I taste something metallic. When I pull my hand away, I see blood on it. What? Then I feel a gush from my nose and blood splashes down onto my chest.

I sense my legs coming out from under me and then I'm looking into Davis' eyes again. He catches me and holds me like a baby. Davis' eyes look scared. He starts walking to the front door.

"Biz, you're bleeding."

I want to say "I know," but instead I say, "Jules… In Bedroom," right before my world goes black.

Chapter 19-Present: Biggest Surprise of All

I'm on a bed, but the bed is moving fast. It's the only description I have for the sensation I'm experiencing as I come to. I start to sit up and am stopped by a hand on my shoulder. I know the touch. It's one I haven't felt in a while.

"Davis?" I ask as his face comes into view above me.

Davis squats down so he's face to face with me.

Looking around, I continuing my questions, "Are we in… in an ambulance?"

The space between Davis' eyebrows pinches together. "Yes." He sounds like he can't believe I'm even asking this question.

"Why? I feel fine."

Davis cradles the side of my head in his hand, "Don't you remember what happened." He rubs my head gently with his thumbs.

My thoughts and words start to come fast and frantic. "Yeah, Randall…" And then with actual joy, I proclaim, "We got him!" Davis is nodding his head rapidly and making soothing shushing sounds. My emotions switch again to concern, "Donovan… he got shot. Is Donovan okay?"

"He's on his way to the hospital. It looks terrible, but he swears it's 'fucking nothing.'" Davis imitates Donnie's gruff voice when he says the last part.

I let go a chest full of anxiety with a long sigh and then keep talking, "And Jules, what happened to Jules? Oh my God! Please tell me she's okay."

Davis smiles tightly and then Jules' face appears over his shoulder, "I'm fine. A little shaken up but fine." Jules really does look fine. Pale, but fine.

"The baby?" I ask fearfully.

She puts a hand on Davis' shoulder and one on her belly, "He's doing great."

"It's a boy?" I ask without thinking.

"Shit!" Jules laughs, "I wasn't supposed to tell."

Tears of relief flood my eyes. Jules is fine. The baby is fine.

If everything is okay, why am I being transported in an ambulance? I bring my hand up to wipe away my tears. Why is there blood on my hand? I bring the other one up to join it in front of my face. It's bloody, too. There is blood all down my arms. I feel fine. I can't have been shot, can I?

I sit up with a start and begin the barrage of questions again. "Davis, what's going on? Why am I covered in blood?"

Davis' expression shifts to relieved and confused as he whispers, "I'm so glad you're awake. I'm so glad you're chattering." But he hasn't answered my question.

I feel a squeeze on my other arm and look up. An EMT is taking my blood pressure and he answers my question, "Ms. Brandon. You had a massive hemorrhage from your nose and then you passed out."

I'm incredulous. "Massive hemorrhage? From my nose? You mean… a nosebleed? I've never had a nosebleed in my life."

The EMT qualifies, "It was pretty severe. You lost consciousness. And you witnessed two people being shot…" The scene at the condo begins to replay in my head, clearing up any confusion or slowness of thought I'd just experienced.

"But I feel fine!" I protest.

Davis and Jules surround me, each holding me with both hands somewhere. Davis runs a hand through my hair. The feeling calms me more than the shushing.

"Shhh. Good, Lizard baby. It's so good that you feel fine, but it looks like you lost a lot of blood. We just need to get you checked out."

The ambulance stops moving. I assume we are at the emergency room, which is not far from our condo. The EMTs ask me to lie back down, which I do, and they start preparing to move me. One of them, not the one that took my blood pressure, tells Davis, "Mr. Brandon, when we get your wife in, you'll need to go to the registration desk while we get her settled."

Davis opens his mouth to disagree, when Jules pipes up, "I'll go with her Davis. You take care of all that paperwork stuff. She'll be all cleaned up when you get back to her."

He tells me, "I don't want to leave you!"

I say softly to reassure him, "It's okay. I look terrible. Go!"

"Terrible? You're the best thing I've seen in weeks." Davis motions for the EMTs to hold up on moving me. "I love you, Lizard. I'll be right there, okay?"

"Okay," I mouth and nod my head that it's okay for him to leave. I have a bunch of questions I want to ask Jules in private anyway.

***

"He told me he'd been in your condo plenty of times. He'd been sneaking in through the garbage chute and picking your lock." As Jules helps me into a hospital gown and hands me wet washcloths to clean up, she describes how she, and Randall, came to be in my guest room. "I had just unlocked the door to your apartment to bring you some flowers and be there when you got home, 'cause you seemed kind of tired and sad. As I pushed the door open, I was shoved inside. I was so pissed and when I finally twisted myself around, Randall was right there, stinking of trash and sneering at me. He grabbed my arm and dragged me to the guest room. God, I was so scared. All I could think of was, 'How could I call someone? How could I dial my phone without him knowing.' I didn't have a chance. He took my cell phone, tied me to the chair and taped my mouth. After that he didn't do anything to me. Ignored me really. He was just texting on my phone like a madman and pacing until you arrived."

My blonde upbeat friend has been so brave. I don't see a chink in her emotional armor right now. I would be a blubbering mess! I *am* a blubbering mess as I tell her, "I'm so sorry that happened to you and so glad that you're okay. Don't you need to get checked out?"

"Really, I'm good. The EMTs examined me. Charlie is on his way. I'm more worried about you." Ever organized, in control, in charge Jules. I'm so blessed she's my friend.

"Donovan?" As I blurt out the question, I feel guilty, like I have inappropriately forgotten to be concerned.

Jules is going to go find out more about him as soon as Davis gets back. The nurse that gave me the gown and helped me get onto the ER bed returns. Her name is Doris. She has warm, kind eyes and a Jamaican accent, which is unusual for this part of the country. It's very soothing. Doris takes my vitals, asks me a ton of questions, some of them personal, including the dreaded, "Are you pregnant?" one.

I tell her it would be impossible. We've been trying for over three years and I've only been with my husband for one week over the past ten.

Doris tilts her head to the side, smiles and replies, "Stranger tings *have* happened, Ms. Brandon."

Doris informs me she'll need a urine sample anyway. When I ask why, she says it's routine and that I'll also be having some blood work. I feel ridiculous. It was just a bloody nose.

***

"Okay, you're all registered," Davis says flatly upon entering the exam room.

That is Jules' cue and she leaves to go find out more about Donnie. I hope they'll tell her something, with all the privacy laws there are now for patients. Maybe one of the other policemen will know something.

"I'll be back soon," Jules says and then giggles, "Give you guys a chance to get reacquainted." I'm pleased to see when she exits, it's with the usual Jules bounce in her walk.

I'm finally alone with Davis and I suddenly feel so shy. We lock eyes and I give him a small smile. Davis' head cocks to one side. His green eyes that I love so much glimmer, "Hi, Lizard. Hi, Baby," he whisper shouts as he walks up to me and folds me in his arms. I push my face into his chest and inhale deeply. He smells like home. I didn't realize how much I'd missed him, his presence, his smell, how our house seemed empty until just his second.

I stop sniffing and tilt my head up so my chin is on his chest, "Hi, Mavis. I missed you so much. We don't ever have to do that again, do we? Tell me. Never Again."

"Never *ever* again." Davis says meaningfully. Then he leans down and kisses me. A soft, full kiss that instantly takes me back to our first kiss, the first time we made love. The zap. The buzz. A feeling down low in my belly I only associate with being close to Davis.

"'Scuse me." My nurse, Doris, is back. "I'm sorry to interrupt. Ms. Brandon, I need to get some blood. And the doctor will be in soon to examine you."

While Doris is setting up to take blood, Jules returns. She appears to be out of breath when she comes back in the room. "Hey…Umm… they wouldn't let me see him. Detective Garrett. But I did run into his wife, Posey. Wow! She is adorable. And his two boys. Did you know he had kids?" I nod yes and wave my hands toward myself, motioning her to tell me how Donnie is. To give me something. I feel like she's avoiding telling me the truth.

"He's in surgery."

I feel my eyebrows raise. "Really?"

Jules comes over and stands by the end of my bed, "Biz, it's not good. He was shot in the left shoulder. And his wife said there are lots of arteries… So, she says she doesn't know too much yet… they are still waiting to hear from the surgeon."

The last I remember, Donnie was sitting on the floor, wounded, but conscious and holding a gun on Randall. He was directing Davis what to do and then…I don't remember hearing him talk again after he told me to look out and I turned around.

"If you're okay, I'm going to go back and sit with Mrs. Garrett… Posey." Jules' words yank me back to the present.

I encourage her to go, "Oh, yeah, I mean, YES! Go. Please go stay with her. I'm fine. Davis is here." Suddenly, I wince and rub Davis' hand and look at him to distract my attention from Doris sticking me with a needle.

Not long after Jules leaves the doctor comes and examines me. I don't remember him introducing himself but his badge says, Dr. Kennedy. He is joined by Doris and a female police officer, who introduces herself with her last name only – Carpenter. The doctor looks up my nose. Down my throat. Asks me how I'm feeling. Do I have a headache? I report to him that I really feel okay. Davis stands next to me through the entire examination, never releasing my hand.

Then the doctor asks very slowly, "Ms. Brandon, I'm going to ask your husband to leave for a few minutes."

"Why?" I'm baffled. I don't want Davis to leave. I have nothing to hide from him.

Officer Carpenter, who has said nothing so far, interjects, "The doctor needs to examine you further…"

"But I'm fine," I protest. "I didn't get raped, if that's what you think. Randall threatened me and pushed me around, but nothing hap…"

The office cuts me off, "It's procedure, Ms. Brandon. We don't want to miss any evidence. You *were* attacked. This is important. I also need to take your preliminary statement tonight." She turns to Davis. "Mr. Brandon. There is an officer outside waiting to speak with you also."

Davis looks the female officer square in the eyes "I'm not leaving her."

I squeeze his hand and he directs his attention back to me. "Davis. Go. Go talk to the officer. This will be over soon. Let's do this right so Randall can't possibly hurt anyone else."

Davis scowls.

"Your wife is right, Mr. Brandon," Officer Carpenter tells him.

Davis sighs in mock defeat, "She generally is." Leaning down he says, "I'm continually impressed by how brave you are, Lizard." He kisses my forehead, my nose and finally my lips. When he stops kissing he says, "I'll be right back."

The doctor's examination is not unlike going to the gynecologist, except everything he does is carefully monitored by Doris and Officer Carpenter. It's uncomfortable and I'm not unaware of how harrowing this could be for someone that was *really* sexually assaulted. I know how I felt after Randall supposedly raped me years ago. And that, evidently, wasn't even a "completed" assault. I give the police officer my statement during the exam. My level of calmness is freaky. Where did my nuclear-level panic go?

Dr. Kennedy finishes and tells my nurse that Davis can return. She opens the door a crack and tells Davis it's okay. He is by my side in a flash.

The doctor is turned away from us, washing his hands. Right before he and the others leave, he says he'll look at my labs and see if I need an IV or more tests. If it all checks out I can probably leave soon.

Davis' phone rings in his pocket. He pulls it out, tells me it's Charlie and answers, "Hey, Boxwood. Yes, she's fine." Davis points at me. "Uh, yeah… she's here." Davis points out the door and mouths, 'Jules,' effectively telling me what Charlie's question was. "Hmm, weird. Well, she's sitting with Donovan Garrett's wife. He was shot by Randall at the condo. We don't know. Waiting to hear. No, no, Randall isn't here. He's at University Hospital across town. In handcuffs. With a guard outside his door, I'm sure. He shot a fucking cop! Yeah, I think he's going away for a long time. The other charges are nothing compared to this." That answers that question. Randall's whereabouts were invading my thoughts about every three seconds, but I didn't want to ask out loud. Davis is pacing around the room as he talks about Randall. Then his tone changes and he says, "I know. I will, man. Oh, okay. I'll walk down there and tell her to call you. K. Bye."

Davis hangs up with Charlie and says, "Jules isn't answering her phone. I'm going to walk down there and tell her to call Charlie. He'll be here soon. I'll find out about Donovan, too. Okay?"

I answer, "Yes. Absolutely. Go tell Jules and come back and tell me how Donnie's doing. I bet the doctor will be back soon. I'm fine. I'm sure of it. I bet I'll be dressed and ready to go by the time you get back." I wave Davis out of the room.

Davis turns in the doorway and adds, "Your brother said to tell you he loves you." Davis eyebrows almost hit his hairline. Charlie doesn't say stuff like that often, so it's something big. Charlie. My "brother." It puts a big smile on my face. My first smile since this ordeal began.

***

The doctor comes back. There IS a reason for the passing out and the nosebleed. It's shocking news. Unexpected, unbelievable, SCARY news. I make the doctor promise not to say anything to Davis. I want to break it to him myself – at home.

By the time Davis is back. I'm sitting on the edge of the exam table, fully dressed with my discharge papers in hand. I tell him everything is fine. Just a fluke nosebleed. I start pummeling him with questions about Donovan, because I want to know. And I want to deflect his attention from me. He tells me we can talk about it in the car.

"Ready to leave?" he asks.

I reply happily, "Never more. Let's go home."

"Yeeeessssss. I miss my bed." Davis stretches and rubs his back. "Hotel beds suck."

"That's all you miss?" I tease.

"THAT we'll talk about at home. In bed." Davis teases back as he wraps an arm my waist, cupping my hip. He looks down at me and kisses me softly and slowly in a non-verbal "Hello." The emergency room noise floats away. I can see nothing. Hear nothing but him.

And the little voice in my back of my head asking how I'm going to break the news.

Chapter 20-Present: Driving Home

"So, Donnie's out of surgery. Fortunate son of a bitch, I've got to say. The bullet somehow missed any major arteries. Narrowly. He's going to have a fucked up shoulder, though. Maybe permanently. But he's alive. I don't know how Posey Garrett does it. She's a strong woman."

I sigh with relief as Davis catches me up about Donnie. "We can visit him tomorrow?" I ask.

Davis nods his head affirmatively, "Yes, Posey thought that would be fine. Jules was going to stay with her a bit longer, then go home. Charlie got there just as I was leaving. He was going to come see you, but I told him to take his pregnant wife home and call you tomorrow. There's just too much going on."

"Oh my God! I have to call my parents! Your parents!" I wonder if they know by now. Davis tells me he already called his parents, but only to assure them we were both fine before any of it was reported in the news.

As I start to dial my parents, I question Davis, "Do you think it will make the news soon?" My phone chirps and the text answers my question. "Never mind," I say. It's a heads-up from Kathleen. Being a member of the media, she has the inside track on how the news will be reported. I read it aloud to Davis.

> Prepare yourselves. The headlines tomorrow will read something like this:
>
> "Connelly-Brandon 'Fake-Up' All An Act to Catch Alleged Rapist Ireland."

"'Fake-Up,' huh? Clever," is all Davis says.

My mother answers on the first ring and I spend the rest of our drive home, right up until we get through our front door, explaining (apologizing) about the faux separation and the sting. Only when I agree to call first thing in the morning and visit soon does my mother agree to end the call.

I do have to call her in the morning. I will have told Davis by then and I'll need to tell my folks soon after.

After I say good-bye for the third time to her, she yells out, loud enough for Davis to hear, "Take care of her, Davis!"

Davis yells at the phone in my hand, because he heard her from a few feet away, "I will, Diane."

"I love you both."

Davis and I reply in unison, "We love you."

Only then does she hang up.

Chapter 21-Present: So Into You

"Ugh, I feel so gross. If it's okay with you I'm going to go wash off and change." The only thing I'm wearing that's my own is my underwear, since it and my bra were all I was wearing when Donnie and Davis rescued me. The hospital gave me a pair of scrubs and footie socks to wear home. My bra is the lone object in the personal possessions bag I'm holding, along with my discharge papers. I hope my phone is somewhere in this condo, because I can't for the life of me remember where it is. I should probably ask Davis to call it.

Before I can even do that, I look around the condo and release an anguished moan. The place is wrecked. The police have been here, I can tell. There are bloodstains from Donnie and Randall that are partially cleaned up, but the sofa and furniture are in disarray. There are also wrappers and remnants of medical supplies on the floor, I guess from the EMTs working on them both.

Davis comes up behind me, wraps his arms around me and tells me evenly, "I think that's a brilliant idea. It's been a long night. The sun will be up soon. You go take a shower or bath, whatever you want. I'll clean up in here and when you're done, I'll put you to bed."

"*Put* me to bed?" I ask as I lean back into his embrace.

"You need to rest. You've been through a huge trauma. You look whipped."

I reply sarcastically, "Thanks."

"Sorry. It's true. You look tired…" I wonder if he already knows. How could he know? He doesn't know. I'm just messing with my own head.

"Sorry I was crabby. I *am* tired. And we both have to give more complete statements to the police tomorrow."

Davis spins me around to face him. "Ugh... I was avoiding talking about that."

Davis kisses me and then spins me back around to face the bedroom. He says, "Go!" and then smacks me on the bottom.

I jump and shoot him a smile over my shoulder, "Yes, Sir."

As I shut the bedroom door, Davis adds, "I'll be in soon"

***

I walk directly to the tub and turn on the water for a bath. Standing in a shower feels like too much work. Stripping the hospital scrubs and my panties off and cramming them into the laundry hamper, I stand buck naked in front of the vanity mirror. The reflection is of my whole body from the top of my head to my hipbones. I stare at myself disbelieving. How do I tell him? How do I tell Davis the news I received at the hospital? I run my hands down the sides of my waist and then wrap them slowly around myself, stopping briefly over my belly. I'm struck by the perfect idea. I think I might have just what I need to tell him without saying a word . Oh man, I hope I didn't throw them all out. Still completely naked, I scramble around in the drawers of the vanity.

Got it!

I follow the directions and then walk away from the vanity. Sinking into the tub, now almost overflowing with warm, comforting water, I let my mind drift.

***

Knock, knock, knock!

I startle and sit bolt upright in the tub. Water pours out everywhere, sloshing tidalwave-esque over the sides, flooding the bathroom floor.

"Hey, Lizard. Are you okay?" Davis' concerned voice carries easily through the bathroom door.

"Uh, yeah." My voice sounds groggy.

"Then why is the door locked? Why have you been in there so long?"

"It hasn't been that long," is what I'm about to say, but then I raise a hand in front of my face and see it is really pruny.

After a moment, I realize Davis is waiting for me to answer, "I, umm, I'll be right out. I fell asleep in the tub."

"Okay," Davis says. I hear him walking away from the door. His voice is less loud so I know he's walked back into our bedroom. "Just maybe don't lock the door when you're in the tub. Especially when you're so tired."

I reply, "K," and then get out of the tub.

The bedroom is completely dark, except for Davis' bedside light, when I open the door from the bathroom. I walk, wrapped in a towel into the closet under the pretext of getting into my PJs. I'm really there to deliver something to Davis' sock drawer. I write the information Davis will need in the future on the corner of the discharge paperwork and place it with the object from the bathroom in the drawer.

"Come to bed, Lizard Baby. I need some sleep and so do you."

I increase my speed, throw off the towel and rake on my old favorite sleepwear, my Hello Kitty PJ pants and a black tank top.

"I know." I walk nonchalantly into the bedroom and produce a partially manufactured yawn. "I'm here." Sliding into bed and skootching right up next to him, I kiss Davis' chest. He kisses the top of my head, then reaches over and shuts off his light.

"I'll see YOU in the morning." He husks into my ear. He's not talking about *seeing* me.

I yawn and move in closer, "Not if I see YOU first."

***

I can't sleep. I get up two times and use the bathroom. When I come back to bed each time, I snuggle back into Davis' side, but the sleep still won't come. I just keep replaying the whole evening and the weeks preceding over and over in a loop in my mind. I know I can breathe easier now, even though there will be another trial and even bigger changes ahead for us. I just can't seem to settle down. And it's not like I'm having a panic attack. It doesn't feel like that. In fact, I'm calm. I just have so much to process.

Davis' voice breaks the silence in the darkness, "Why aren't you asleep?"

"I'm sorry. I didn't mean to wake you up." I turn my head to look up at him. I can't see him well in the blackness.

Davis sits up and I move with him. He flips his bedside light on. There he is. My gorgeous green-eyed husband. "You didn't. I never fell asleep. I couldn't. I just wanted to hold you and listen to you breathe. You're so restless. Are you okay?"

I sit up more and shift to face him, looking at his chest and arms as he leans against our headboard. "I can't turn my mind off."

Davis sighs, reaches out and takes my hand. "I completely understand," he says. Then he rubs my knuckles with his thumb and all the questions I want to ask him – what happened to him while we were apart, what will happen with Randall, WHY he was dating Suzette – all fall away. Instead I'm filled with need, in my heart and in the deepest most intimate places of my body.

In an unspoken signal, as soon as I look up from the place where he's touching me and our eyes meet, we are both up on our knees and locked in an embrace. Meeting each other again in the middle of our bed. Our sanctuary.

"Oh my God, I missed you. I missed you so much," Davis tells me between kisses.

Our lips cannot be stopped. I want to kiss and taste every inch of him. "Mavis, Baby… I missed YOU."

We stop kissing and our foreheads touch. Our breathing rough and ragged. I begin to chatter frantically, "Davis, we should talk. I need to know things. I… I need to tell you something…"

Davis chuckles, "That's it. No more. As much as I love your chatter, I don't want to talk right now. I just want you. ONLY you. That's all I need."

"But that's what…" and then Davis' mouth covers mine. There is no way I can argue further. The buzz, the zap, the feeling I had the first time I met him and every time I'm near him overtakes any rational thought. We are the equivalent of atoms that are physically unable to resist each other.

Davis' tongue parts my lips powerfully. He runs his tongue under my upper lip and then bites it gently. I nip back. Then I stroke his tongue with mine. I swear we are trying to touch every part of each other, as we come together and part briefly, only to allow a tank top, pair of boxer briefs or panties to fly off our bodies.

Completely naked, facing each other, Davis kisses down my neck, across my collar bone. One of his hands comes up to cup a breast and scrape his deliciously rough thumb across by rock hard nipple. I moan and push into his thumb, trying to feel more. My own hands slide across his lats and down to his waist. My thumbs circle, brushing forward to explore the deep V that leads down to his ever-hardening cock.

Davis takes the opposite nipple into his mouth with pulsing suckles. My hands slide up his body and into his dark silky hair, pulling it closer to me, begging him to possess me. He moves from my breast and kisses down my stomach to one of my hipbones and then stops suddenly when he's about to move lower.

"What's this?" he points to the place his lips just left, slightly to the right of my hip and down a bit.

I'd almost forgotten. The tattoo. The one I got right after our "fake-up" began. The one that says my favorite thing.

Have Fun.

I act like I don't know what he's talking about and tease him, "What?"

His finger brushing over it he asks, "Is this a tattoo?"

"Yes," I say with a "duh!" in my tone. "It's a tattoo. And, sort of… directions, all in one."

Davis reads the tattoo out loud and then looks up at me from his low angle. "HAVE FUN? Well, all I can say to that is, 'Yes, Ma'am! Your wish is my command.'" Before I can say a word or tease him further, Davis has scooped me up under my knees, laid me flat on my back and has begun to attend to the place at the apex of my thighs. He exhales a hot, needy breath right over my clit and then licks it lightly, increasing the pressure and frequency each time. I'm already aching for release, poised on the edge, so it doesn't take long before I feel the ramping up and flooding, vibrating release. Practically indecipherable, "Oh, oh, ooooooh my God" repeatedly escapes my quivering lips. My fingers claw at Davis's shoulders and hair.

I'm panting, coming off the high of my eye-clenching orgasm, just as I feel Davis move up over me and plunge his greedy cock deep into me. It pushes all the air out of me in an "Oof."

"Jesus, Biz… Lizard. How is it possible that you feel better than I ever remember?" he asks.

I can only answer honestly, "Because I'm still so into you. Everything about you. Ever since I met you. I only feel this way because of you. Always will."

Davis thrusts into me and I match him with each one. He comes with a satisfied growl and I join him, coming for the second time tonight.

Chapter 22-Present: Sock Drawer

"Hey," Davis says.

I'm in the walk-in closet, shuffling things around in his sock drawer. Really, just convincing myself that the things I put in there are real and not from my imagination. Last night, all of it, was so surreal!

Turning my head, I see he is right behind me taking up the entire doorway. His arms up, hands grasping the top of the doorframe and leaning in. I can make out every muscle in his arms and chest through his plain black t-shirt. Hmm. Plain t-shirt. That's unusual. I wonder why he's not wearing one of his t-shirts designed to make me smile.

"You're organizing my sock drawer. What's stressing you out? What are you hiding?" Davis asks as he comes up behind me and presses his firm chest to my back. Davis wraps one arm around my waist. I back myself into him slightly, turn my head and rest my cheek on his collarbone. Maybe it's me that can make *him* smile.

"Nothing," I whisper.

Davis leans over my shoulder and grabs the plastic object and the piece of paper I was about to replace in his sock drawer.

Davis jokes, "You mean *this* nothing?"

As much as I love being this close to him. I need to give him a minute to really see what is in his hand. I duck out of his embrace and back up until I hit the side of the doorway with my butt, which stops me.

Davis doesn't try to stop me. He's too busy looking at the off-white plastic stick in his hand and then the paper and then back at the stick. Confusion sweeps over his face and his eyebrows pinch together. Slowly he turns and asks, his voice cracking, "Is this true? Does this mean what I think it does?"

I smile broadly and nod yes. "Davis... Mavis, I told you I'd never hide anything from you again, I just didn't know how to tell you because I could barely believe it myself." Then I say the word out loud that I haven't been able to wrap my head around since the doctor told me last night. "I'm pregnant!"

"Really?" Davis moves toward me, brows raised, grinning in disbelief.

I want to jump into his arms, so I do. "Look at the stick. Read the paper. We're going to have a baby!"

Davis scoops me up and swings me around, then placing me back against the door jam, he drops to his knees. Davis pulls my tank top up, grabs my butt with his other hand and pulls my body close to his mouth. He speaks into my belly button. "Hey, little baby, it's your Dad. I cannot tell you how excited I am you decided to choose us to be your parents..."

I can't stop the tears winding down my face, over my nose and splashing into Davis' hair. At last, not tears of fear, anger or panic. Tears of absolute unrelenting happiness.

"What's with the locksmith number on the discharge paper?" Davis asks, not looking up from my tummy. He's actually nuzzling and kissing it, making me feel anything but maternal.

I laugh out loud. He DID see the number I wrote down. "Remember, you said when we had kids we'd have to get locks on the doors. I thought you might want to get a jump on that. You know so we have some privacy and can still make out in the closet..."

"Yep, I remember. I'm going to get right on that. But first, I think I'll quiet your chatter right here in the closet one last time, without locks!"

Davis lays me down right there on the wall-to-wall carpet. The squirrel chatter stops immediately.

The End.
Have Fun.

Epilogue: The following February

I really didn't mind being pregnant. Let me rephrase. I really didn't mind being pregnant after the unorthodox way I found out and the first trimester. I can't say I enjoyed the barfing, but it was comforting for the seven and a half months I knew I was pregnant, to always have a little bit of Davis with me. When the baby started moving, I knew I would never be alone again. Davis became even more protective than he already was. Oh, and I got to eat anything I wanted, except sushi and lunch meat, and "oh yeah, try to cut down on the caffeine." Probably the hardest part.

I did mind delivery. Don't let your friends fool you. It's uncomfortable and before the epidural, (Yes, I had an epidural because I'm a wimp and proud of it), painful. It hurt so bad I called Davis a "motherfucker" during a long squirrel-like rant, right before I got it. It's not a word I typically use. He wasn't offended.

He just laughed and smiled his sexy, smirky smile and told me, "Yes, I know… I believe that's how we got here."

The anesthesiologist had to stop and tell me to quit moving, so he could place the needle, I was laughing so hard. Davis was right. That's exactly how we got here.

Here is in one of the Labor-Delivery-Recovery rooms at Barnes Hospital. I'm exhausted from delivering our baby and drifting in and out of sleep. Davis has been great. I haven't even changed a diaper.

During one of my "drifts out," I look down to see and feel Davis' hand in my hand and his arm across my now much flatter stomach. I look up his arm to see him sitting next to my bed, turned away from me, his chin resting on his other hand, which is propped on the edge of a clear hospital bassinet. Davis is sitting very still and watching, just watching, our newborn son sleep. Like he sometimes watches me.

"Hey," I say, rubbing my fingers over the back of his hand.

Davis turns just his face to look up and slightly back at me. He still leans on the bassinet.

His voice is soft and full of emotion, "Hi, Lizard Baby."

"What are you doing?" I ask.

Davis sighs happily, "Just looking at him. Trying to figure out what he looks like. What name he looks like."

Davis and I have already briefly discussed that "Cole," Davis' brother's name, could be part of our son's name. I figured it would be his first name, so I didn't really consider many others for too long. I was thinking Cole Davis or Cole James.

I quietly question, "What about Cole for the first name?"

"He doesn't look like a Cole." Davis has turned back to his original position gazing at our son.

"What does he look like?"

Davis reaches out one finger of his hand and strokes our baby's little soft pink hand, "I can't quite put my finger on it. I've run through a hundred or so options, but just can't figure it out. Do we even have a baby name book?"

"No," I reply, "I just looked on Goo…" I stop myself from saying Google, "on-line."

Davis turns to me, shaking his head and laughing softly into his upper arm. The word Google always makes him smile. He looks once again at our beautiful boy and then back at me. He's still holding my hand, rubbing his thumb across my knuckles.

Davis, pinning me with his green guy-linered eyes, the ones that stole my heart, says, "I just can't believe how crazy lucky I am."

I inhale audibly. My husband is a genius. I guess the sound I just made sounded like pain, because Davis is now on his feet, leaning over me with a very concerned look on his face. "Are you okay?"

"I… I'm fine. I just had a moment. Say that last thing you said again."

Slowly he says, "Uh, I can't believe how crazy lucky I am?"

"Yeah, that's it. That's his name."

"Crazy?"

I squeeze Davis' hand, cock my head, purse my lips duck-like, bug out my eyes and finally say, "No, smarty-pants. Lucky."

"Lucky?"

"Yeah, Lucky. I'd like to name him Lucky."

Davis tries the name out, "Lucky Brandon. Yeah. I like it."

I correct him, "Lucky *Cole* Brandon."

Davis releases my hand, turns and picks up sleeping Lucky. He tells him, "We're going to call you Lucky, big guy, because you are the result of all our luck. Finding each other, healing each other, loving each other. We got Lucky."

Soft tears roll down my cheeks as Davis hands me our son.

Lucky makes a few squeaky sounds.

"Hey, he has a hamster snore, just like his mom," Davis proclaims, as he crawls into bed next to us. Our little three-person family, cuddling for the first time.

***

Davis yells at me through the door to the bathroom in my hospital room, "Okay, I've got him all dressed. We're ready to leave."

I turn off the blow dryer and am doing one final brushing of my hair. I'm still a little sore from delivery, but I think I look presentable enough for the short ride home. And I do mean short. The hospital is only four blocks from our condo.

I collect the last of my toiletries and put them in my large make-up travel bag, while I yell back, "Did you put him in the outfit I put out?"

Pushing the bathroom door open and looking at them both standing in front of me I see that Davis did NOT put Lucky in the going away outfit I chose.

Davis announces "We came up with something better."

He holds Lucky up, "Lion King Style" in front of me. Lucky is wearing a black onesie with white stitching with the words MOM LOVES ME on it. I forgive Davis immediately for the baby's wardrobe change.

"Awwwww," I coo.

Davis hands Lucky off to me and says, "Check out mine."

Davis stands back and spreads his arms out to the side.

"Awwww," I say again, "Matching t-shirts."

Davis shakes his head and presses his lips together, controlling a chuckle, "Not *quite*. There's a subtle difference... Read mine again."

I stare at his shirt again and it hits me. They are *almost* the same, except where Lucky's says MOM LOVE*S ME*, Davis' says:

MOMS LOVE ME

Laughing so loud, it momentarily startles Lucky, I confess, "They sure do."

I walk over to Davis and let him wrap both of us in his strong, but gentle embrace. I lean my face up and Davis' lips cover mine, slowly opening them and kissing me so deeply, my insides contract and release over and over. Lucky wriggles in my arms.

Davis breaks the kiss, but keeps his face very close to mine, holding me in his gaze. He reaches over and strokes Lucky's hair.

I ask, "The t-shirts? It's going to be a thing with you two, isn't it?

Davis answers, "Already is. Gotta keep Mommy smiling."

Lucky Mom.

Lucky's Mom.

Like I said right before Davis first said he loved me, when I thought he was talking about someone else.

The girl that Davis loves?

Lucky Girl.

Acknowledgments:

Thank you:

Sharon Korn, my editor. Thanks for going on this journey for a third time.

Sarah Hansen at Okay Creations. Thank you for making the cover of Still Into You and the whole Better Than Series so beautiful.

Jennifer Stevens

My Beta readers: Cathy A., Brian, Barb, Nikki, Kelly, Kevin and Julie.

The authors and bloggers:

Jamie McGuire (just get used to this Thank You in every book)-for your FAQs for Writers page on your website.

Isabelle Peterson-Big Love, my friend.

Liv Morris-Ya Know What I Mean?

Erica Cope

Rachel Robinson

Tali Alexander and Chapter One Live! on YouTube.

Fictional Boyfriends, Pixie's Book Blog, Maryse's Book Blog, Amazeballs Book Addicts, Rude Girl Book Blog, Book Boyfriend Reviews, A Risque Affair Book Blog, Love Between the Sheets, Just One More Page, Cecily's Book Review, The Book Lover's, and Smutty Book Friends.

And any of the other bloggers I've missed in these acknowledgements. You help indie authors everyday. You are so appreciated.

All the Ladies (and Gent of AS101). You know who you are. I depend on you – daily.

To BC and The Connor Boys – Get out of my spot! I need to write.

About the Author

Emme Burton is the author of the new adult novels Better Than Me, and Fix It For Us. She lives in St. Louis, Missouri with her amazing husband, two teenage sons, and her "fur boy." Emme has never, ever been lost in a mall either as a child or an adult. Her mother, and now her family, have always known where to find her. At the bookstore.

Like Emme's Facebook Page: Author Emme Burton

And *Follow* her on Twitter: @EmmeBurton

www.ingramcontent.com/pod-product-compliance
Lightning Source LLC
Chambersburg PA
CBHW021919170626
46807CB00007B/2903